The
Black
Crescent

J.N. Jamieson

Cover by Elizabeth Mackey

ISBN: 978-1-7365336-1-1

Table of Contents

THE SEA RESCUERS

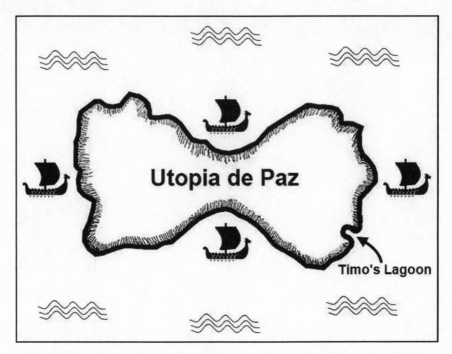

The Island of Utopia de Paz — Viking longships surround the Utopian coastline on four sides to prevent escape. Timo's hidden lagoon lies on the southeast side of the island.

Chapter 1

Mountainous seas towered over the tiny ship as the skipper fought the wheel to steer the course. Another wave of green water crashed over the bow, bending the forward rail inward like a crushed tin can. A massive dragon head on a slender neck rose from the sea, hovering over the vessel, red eyes gleaming like red-hot coals.

In desperation, the terrified captain tried to turn the boat, but she failed to respond. The monster's mouth gaped, fangs glistening as the serpent's head plunged into the sea, swallowing its prey in a single gulp. Darkness descended upon the crew as they screamed in terror. Screams no one else could hear . . .

The emergency alarm shrieked like a banshee, waking Coast Guard Rescue Skipper Jim McGraw from the nightmare. He rolled out of the hard cot, planting his feet on the deck as he cursed the inventor of the maddening, but effective wake-up torture device.

Not that it mattered. The nightmares each night kept him awake anyway, tossing and turning until dawn. He reached over and slapped the switch to turn off the high-pitched squeal, glancing at the lime-green glow of the digital clock. Two o'clock in the morning?

This would be his third rescue case since his watch began yesterday morning. He pulled on his dark blue shirt, pants and boots, grabbed his jacket and stepped out into the humid night. Not a breath of wind tonight, typical of summer at the Shell Beach Search and Rescue station on Florida's west coast. Jim hurried down to the docks to his rescue boat moored at the end near the canal entrance.

The rumble of the twin diesels greeted him, as did the faint odor of diesel exhaust. JT, his engineer, already had the engines raring to go. Popping his head out of the engine compartment, the young mechanic waved and said, "Morning there, Skip. Busy night so far. Any idea where we're headed this time?"

Jim waved and replied, "Not yet. About to call the comms center, JT. I'll let you know."

He stepped aboard and into the pilothouse, tossing his gear into a corner, and called the base radio room for a briefing on the rescue mission. The watch stander said it was a mayday emergency, about ten miles from Shell Beach inlet. They had the vessel's position, but not a lot more.

Big Ben, the deckhand, waved from the bow as he prepared the docking lines and inspected the boat to make sure everything was ready to go. Jim returned the wave as the duty officer, Meyer Stansky, came on the radio. "McGraw, get moving. Communications are in and out, so we'll call you back in a few minutes when we have more info."

Jim signaled Ben to take in the dock lines, backed the rescue craft out of the slip, and headed for the inlet to take them out into the Gulf of Mexico. Stars twinkled overhead and a yellowish full moon rose to the east.

Red and green buoys and beacons flashed on each side of the channel as Jim slowly brought the boat up to full speed. The tiny ship lifted her bow like a hot-blooded stallion as they entered the ocean basin and headed southwest.

Five minutes later, Stansky called back with details. Ben wrote the information into the navigation log as the rest of the crew listened. The *Caroline* was a sixty-five-foot cabin cruiser, drifting about ten miles west of Shell Beach inlet. She had lost engine power.

Four people were aboard. Mom, Dad, and two daughters. One daughter had a fractured arm because a hatch had closed on her when the boat took a roll. Not life threatening, but a break might turn nasty if infection set in or if the bone shifted around. Jim acknowledged the info, sitting back in the helm seat. Not a lot to go on, but that was far from his only concern.

Twenty-four hours out, the weather service predicted that a blockbuster storm may make landfall in either southern Florida or the Gulf of Mexico. The forecasters gave it a 50% chance of coming around the Keys, so the entire state was making preparations, stocking up on emergency supplies, boarding up windows, and moving to evacuation shelters.

But tonight, the ocean was nearly perfect, with a razor-sharp horizon, a canopy of twinkling lights overhead, and shooting stars chasing one another across the sky. Jim recognized the signs of nasty weather after almost fourteen years in the coast guard.

The calm waters, the clear skies, were warnings of howling winds and mountainous seas yet to come. No time for complacency. They needed to find the vessel *Caroline*, rescue the crew and tow her to a safe port ahead of the storm.

Chapter 2

Ben got the towline ready on deck. As he entered the pilothouse, he said, "Swell's getting higher, Skip. Might turn nasty sooner than predicted."

When Ben spoke about anything nautical, Jim's ears perked up. Ben knew his stuff. He was a husky black man, built like a weightlifter, strong, quiet and one of the best sailors Jim had come across. His deckhand grew up helping his dad on a commercial fishing boat, trawling for shrimp in the rough waters off the North Carolina outer banks.

"Well, Ben, let's hope we complete the mission before Mother Nature tosses us around like a bath toy."

The big man nodded. "You got that right. The tow-line's ready. I'll finish up on deck." He stepped back into the night air, shutting the heavy watertight door behind him.

A faint, broken voice came over the radio with lots of static in the background. The speaker crackled and popped, but Jim could not make out what they said. He listened for a few seconds, then tried hailing the distressed cabin cruiser. "Motor Vessel *Caroline*, this is US Coast Guard Rescue 009 on Channel 16 FM, over."

After a brief pause, he called the base to see if they still had communication, but their attempts also produced negative results. Lose comms with a boat in serious trouble and all kinds of funky scenarios start to play out in your head.

Was she taking on water? Had she flooded and sank? Did they have a life-raft? Were they able to transfer the injured woman safely aboard the raft? Abandoning a ship looked easy in the movies, but it was downright dangerous in towering seas and howling winds.

They steamed for another half hour, and Jim tried calling the *Caroline* every five minutes, receiving no response, just light static. Then, they lost all communication with the coast guard base.

JT stepped into the pilothouse after checking the engines and said, "Freezing out there, Skip! Temperature must've dropped over thirty degrees. Crazy weather for June!"

Now, JT was about as opposite personality-wise from Ben as you could imagine. He was a lanky guy with snow-white skin, red hair and freckles everywhere. Jared Taylor Thomas Tecumseh spoke his mind. He was an orphan, raised by his older brother John Phillip deep in the swamps of Louisiana. He loved anything mechanical or electrical. Matter of fact, the engineers on base called him *The Wizard*, a title he'd earned with his reputation as a genius engineer.

JT had the uncanny ability to fix an engine with almost anything, including a paper clip or duct tape. Legend had it he once made a makeshift belt from a pair of women's pantyhose. He knotted the legs together to substitute for a cracked rubber pulley that'd blown off the alternator. His ingenuity got the boat and her crew home in one piece.

Ben rushed into the cabin. "Skip, JT's right. It's cold as a North Carolina winter out there!"

Something wasn't right. Jim told Ben to take the wheel and JT to monitor the radar. Pulling on his foul weather jacket, he opened the door and entered the frigid air, shivering in the night. Forty-degree temperature in June in the Gulf of Mexico?

Using binoculars, he scanned to the left and to the right. Smokey mist surrounded them on all sides, and icy fingers rose from the sea like a crop of head-high corn.

Yelling back to the pilothouse, he said, "JT, check the scope on the two, four, and eight-mile scales. Ben, stop the boat." As the tiny ship slowed to a standstill, Jim strained his eyes through the binoculars, seeing nothing but a hazy horizon.

"Skipper, you'd better take a look at this," shouted JT through the half-open window. Stepping back inside, Jim watched the green glow of the radar, and what he saw made his skin crawl. Four miles ahead, an image appeared as a well-defined line, shaped like an eyebrow, slightly curved in the middle.

Jim went back outside to scan the horizon in the contact's direction. Nothing. Calm, ice-cold, and empty. He yelled back to his engineer, "JT, do you still have the target?"

"Paints clear as a bell, Skip. Four miles off the bow."

"Ben, take her at dead slow speed straight ahead." His helmsman nodded, pushing both throttles into forward gear with one giant hand; the ghostly wall was now only two miles away, painting like a picture on the radar scope, but invisible to the naked eye.

Chapter 3

Jim never put much faith in those old Bermuda Triangle tales, but he figured this might change his mind. He sent Ben to the bow as a lookout and climbed into the helm seat. As their vessel closed in on the eyebrow-shaped contact, steering got harder. Without warning, the wheel froze in place.

Ben shouted back to the pilothouse, pointing to a towering black wall, now visible less than two miles ahead. Jim grabbed the throttles and tried to pull them straight back, but they stayed in gear. The boat revved up to full speed, racing toward the mysterious object in their path.

"JT, engine's not responding and I've lost steering!"

The young mechanic dashed over to the console to fiddle with the controls, then hurried outside to the engine compartment, opened the heavy hatch covers, and jumped inside with his green canvas tool bag.

Thirty seconds later, Jim still could not move the wheel or engine throttles. He dashed out into the ice-cold weather, yelling to Ben to get off the bow and into the cabin.

JT stuck his head out of his engine room. "Skip, you ain't gonna believe this, but the boat's gone bonkers on me. I've pulled the fuel-stop, blocked the air intake, done everything I know, and she's still revving up like a bronco gone crazy!"

Jim told his engineer to leave the engine. JT jumped onto the deck and both men rushed into the pilothouse. Jim shouted, "Okay guys, grab cushions and brace for a collision."

The rescuers held on tight, waiting for impact as the vessel crashed through the wall. But instead of the sound of rending steel, they heard only the swish of the hull as it sliced through the water like a graceful dolphin.

Less than two minutes later, they shot through the darkness into the bright night sky filled with stars and galaxies, so clear it appeared you could reach out and touch the constellations of the heavens.

Balmy temperatures greeted them, the complete opposite of the bone-chilling weather a few minutes earlier. Jim jumped up on the helm seat, grabbed the throttles, pulled them back, and the boat answered his command without hesitation, drifting to a stop.

He rounded her bow up into the gentle breeze, hopped out of the seat, and joined his crew outside. Ahead in the distance, an island rose out of the sea. The silhouette showed high hills or cliffs dotting the landscape. That made no sense because there were no islands in the middle of the Gulf of Mexico. Most of the terrain was flat as a table in this part of the United States.

Fighting to keep calm and confident, Jim said, "JT, give your engines a quick inspection to make sure they're okay. Ben, check the bilges for water."

As soon as his crew departed, he returned to the cabin to check the electronic navigation display, but the device greeted him with a blank screen and no power. Unrolling a nautical chart, he saw empty sea in all directions. Nothing matched the real-time picture outside. With a lump in his throat, he realized he had no idea where they were.

JT popped his head out of the engine room. "Everything's good with the diesels, Skip. No damage and nothing out of sync."

Ben stepped back into the cabin. "Dry as a fish bone in the bilges, Skipper. Not a drop of water anywhere."

Jim nodded, studying the radar, which showed the mysterious island to be about six miles away. It resembled a bow tie or an hourglass lying on its side. He stepped outside for a better look. A full moon appeared as he gazed through the binoculars at the hilly landscape, scanning from side to side. Sandy dunes formed the outer perimeter, with rolling hills or mountains further inland. No shore lights twinkled, and for a fleeting moment, he wondered if they'd come across a remote island in the middle of nowhere.

Jim returned to the pilothouse and tried calling the coast guard station back in Shell Beach, but silence greeted him, cold, dark and quiet.

JT checked the electrical box and shook his head. "Radio's toast and so is the electronic chart plotter, Skip. Guts are burned up on both devices. Strange! We should have sparks all over the place, but they're both cool and dry. Only reason we still have our radar and the depth sounder is they're on a separate power source."

The crew stared at one another, not saying a word, wondering what was going on. What was the black wall they passed through, and where were they? Had they stepped back into another time? As the rescuers were about to discover, that was exactly what happened.

Chapter 4

"Skipper, where'd it go? Where's that crazy black tunnel we just shot through like a cannon ball at warp speed?"

Jim and Ben turned around to see what JT was talking about, and the three men stared into black nothingness behind the boat. Gone! With mouths open, they gazed at an empty sea, twinkling stars, and a spotlight moon, casting glimmering diamonds on the placid ocean.

Jim told the men to stay put as he hurried back into the pilothouse to check the radar. The eyebrow-shaped, mysterious wall astern no longer appeared on the scope, which made zero sense.

He pushed the intercom button overhead. "Both you guys, come on back and let's get moving." As soon as the crew was back inside, he told Ben to take the wheel and gave him a new steering course to the eastern edge of the island.

Jim pulled his cell phone out of the briefcase and stepped outside to connect to a cell tower. No signal. He tossed the device back into his case and turned to his crew. "Okay, guys, here's the plan. We locate an entry point on the eastern side of this island. After we tie up, we find a neighbor who'll let me use their phone to call the base, 'cause I'm getting no reception on my phone. So, let's do it."

This boosted their confidence, but Jim had his doubts about the whole scenario. Everything was so bizarre. What would they find ashore? He said a quick prayer for guidance, shifting his full attention to focus on navigation. His job was to bring his crew home in one piece, no matter the circumstances.

When they were two miles off the beach, they turned north, then northeast, to follow the jagged coastline. Jim studied the radar, looking for indentations that might show an inlet or harbor entrance. Twenty minutes later, a tiny thread of an opening popped up on the scope.

Jim told Ben to stop the boat and then stepped outside. Squinting through his binoculars, he sighted steep banks on the edges of the channel. Bent palm trees lined both sides, their drooping fronds forming an overhead canopy. The inlet might be wide enough to squeeze through, but would it be deep enough?

Jim stuck his head through the open pilothouse window. "Okay JT, you're on the sounder. Call out depths over the intercom. Ben, line her up to stay in the center of the channel. Keep her at dead-slow speed."

They crept inside at a snail's pace as the palm leaves brushed over the top of the mast. JT's twangy voice echoed off the sandy banks, breaking the quiet of the night. "Twenty feet. Seventeen feet. Fourteen feet. Twelve feet and dropping fast, Skip!"

The boat slipped through the narrow neck of the canal into a bowl-shaped lagoon. Moonlight revealed crystal clear water. JT reported, "Six feet, Skip. Holding steady. No change."

Jim clinched his fist over his head to signal Ben to stop the boat. He felt the vessel's engines rumble in reverse as the rescue vessel drifted to a standstill. Now it was time to go ashore and find out where on earth they'd landed.

Chapter 5

With the anchor set deep into the sandy bottom of the lagoon, Jim told JT to wade ashore and tie off the docking lines. He slipped over the side into the waist-high water, draping the lines over his shoulders. After wading ashore, he tied off the ropes to the base of two stout tree trunks. Jim stopped the engine, and all became quiet except for the wind whistling softly through the palm fronds.

Ben and Jim loaded two backpacks with military service pistols, spare ammunition, and emergency flares. Both men carried the bulky equipment to the bow and handed it down to JT. Once all provisions were ashore, the two men entered the warm lagoon water and waded to the tiny sliver of white beach.

The night turned black as a shroud, clouds blotting out the moon and stars. The team strapped on their sidearms, loading their 9 millimeter service pistols with fresh magazines. Switching on his headband light, Jim used his hand compass to lead the way through the dense vegetation of the forest. Ten minutes later, the rescuers came across a clearing occupied by a gray stone cottage.

To one side, a torch flickered, its flame dancing, casting shadows on the sides of the tiny building. The home had a thatched roof, and a narrow cobblestone path led to a wooden door decorated with a lion's head. A massive ring in its mouth served as a knocker.

Jim set his gear down and had the guys stand back, holsters unstrapped and sidearms ready if needed. Who knew who—or what—the rescuers would find? One thing was for sure—this was not Florida in the present day. To him, it looked more like something out of the Middle Ages.

Stepping forward, he tapped the massive knocker and waited. No answer, so he tried again. Finally, the cling and clang of locks and bolts sounded on the opposite side and the door opened. He gazed up at a tallish man in his early seventies, strongly built, with twinkling blue eyes and a kindly, wrinkled face. He was bald except for a fringe of gray hair and a chest-length white beard. The man was dressed in an ankle-length white robe, puffing vigorously on a hand-carved Meerschaum pipe, stuck to one side of his mouth.

In a deep baritone voice, he said, "Well now, you boys hunting bear or barracuda? One thing's for sure, you won't find them here, not on this island. And, you're not invaders, or you'd be clapping me into irons, and I'd sleep in the dungeons tonight."

Invaders? Dungeons? What was he talking about? Jim smiled and said, "Sorry to bother you, sir. We are with the US Coast Guard, and ran into difficulties. I'd like to call our base to let them know where we are. May we use your phone?"

The gentleman with the pipe chuckled and replied, "Don't know what a phone is, but you look innocent enough. If you have a mind to, come inside my humble home and rest for a spell. Come, come." The elderly man stepped aside, gesturing with his pipe hand for the rescuers to enter. "You say you're with the Ghost Guards?"

This was getting weirder by the second. Jim shook his head and said, "Coast Guard, sir. We're a search and rescue team from the base in Shell Beach, Florida. We were on a mission this evening when we became lost, so we moored our boat in the lagoon behind your property. I need to contact our station to inform them of our situation. Does your island have radio communications with the mainland?"

"No, Captain, we have nothing called a radio on the island, either. We are simple people. If we need to communicate, we visit one another on foot or by mule and buggy. All islanders are prohibited from having contact with the mainland. Indeed, it's been like that ever since the invasion, some twenty years ago. But, let's talk more later. You and your men appear weary from your journey. Join me at my table for soup and fresh bread. Call me Timo, an abbreviated version of my birth name, which is Timothy. Please, make yourselves at home."

The rescue crew stood in shocked silence for several seconds, each lost in their thoughts. At the moment, Jim couldn't think of what else to do, so he nodded and said, "Well thank you, sir. We accept your offer."

The rescuers set their gear in a corner of the tiny room and each shook hands with their host as Jim made the introductions.

"Timo, I'm Jim, the skipper; this is Ben, my deckhand, and Jared Thomas, my boat engineer. We nicknamed him JT for short. Where are we and what is the name of your island?"

"Utopia de Paz, or Paradise of Peace. But please, help yourselves to my food, and I will tell you more." Timo passed out stoneware bowls and motioned the men over to the fire. A kettle hung near the hot coals. "The ladle is hanging above the fireplace. I'll cut a few slices of this cracked-wheat bread, fresh from the oven."

They filled their containers to the brim with the steaming stew and returned to join their host. The aroma was intoxicating, a combination of tomato, basil, oregano, rice, onion, and potato chunks. The hungry rescuers straddled the bench and dug in with gusto.

Timo's expression changed from jovial to sullen. He glared at his guests and raised his voice as he shouted, "Stop! What are you doing? Please, wait!" Jim, Ben, and JT held their spoons in midair, looked at one another, and wondered if their eccentric host had lost his mind.

Chapter 6

"Now boys," said Timo, "at my table, we pray before we eat." He pulled an enormous Bible off a wooden stool, blowing the dust off the leather cover, intricately carved with religious scenes. "I hid this under the ashes in the fireplace when the invaders came to my house. Every meal, I recite my favorite prayer from Psalms." He bowed his head, and they followed his lead, reciting the 23rd Psalm: "The Lord is my shepherd; I shall not want . . ."

As Timo concluded, all three crew said in unison, "Amen," picked up their spoons and dug into the delicious bread and stew.

Jim asked, "So, Timo, who are these invaders you mention? And what did they want with you?"

"Well, young man, first I'd like to hear more about my three guests. You're not from around here. Do you live on an island nearby?"

The skipper shook his head. "We are sea rescuers, stationed on the west coast of Florida, and we help people in trouble on the water. Earlier this evening, we left to rescue a vessel named *Caroline*. An hour later, we sighted a mysterious black wall in the sea. It had the shape of an eyebrow or arc. We lost control of our boat as a powerful force pulled us through a dark tunnel to the other side. Afterward, we searched for a place to land, and stumbled across your island, which is not on any of our charts. Crazy as it sounds, that's what happened."

Timo's eyes lit up with excitement as he clasped his hands. "It's true! All these years I've wondered, and now, here you are, Jim. You and your crew are living proof. You found the black crescent? This is fantastic! I studied the writings of the famous Russian scientist, Dimitri Fedorov. In his classic work on time travel, he theorized that once every twenty years, a black curved wall would form in the warm ocean waters near here. On June 7, 1849, the Viking raiders sailed their dragon ships into the Utopian harbor, swarmed ashore, and took over the seaport town. I always suspected they were pulled through the crescent as you described. Your arrival confirms everything. Today is June 7, 1869, exactly twenty years after the invasion. What a miracle!"

All three rescuers' mouths dropped open, speechless. Jim swallowed hard, then said, "Timo, let me get this straight. We've arrived in your world on June 7, 1869? Are you sure of that? Where we came from, the date is June 7, 2029."

Timo replied, "Amazing, but yes, this is true, my friends. But do not worry; you will have no problem returning to your homes. Once the crescent appears, it remains in place for thirty days. The theory states you can travel back and forth as many times as you wish, and you will arrive on each side the same day you left. But you must complete all transits within the thirty-day period. After that, it vanishes for another twenty years."

Big Ben asked. "But Timo, after we passed through, the crescent disappeared. We looked behind us, but it was gone. How do we find it again?"

"Ah yes, Ben, I forgot to mention this. The wall contains a magnetic field, which draws moisture from the sea, forming a thick cloud layer near the surface like a fog bank. When you are pulled through, this depletes part of the energy, which causes rapid evaporation. It takes about twelve hours to recharge and become visible once again. The crescent should be easy to see on your trip back to Shell Beach."

The rescuers sighed with relief after hearing the positive news. Jim said, "So, Timo, tell us more about these Viking invaders."

He puffed on his pipe and said, "They guard the coast day and night with four of their longships to prevent islanders from escaping. In the early days, many Utopians fled to the sea in tiny boats or rafts, but all were caught, taken to the dungeons, and never heard from again." Timo paused, lost in his thoughts, before continuing. "Some of us started an underground resistance group to fight the enemy. We held on for about two years, but in the end, the Viking warriors overwhelmed us."

JT asked, "What happened to the folks who took part in the rebellion, Timo?"

"Well, young man, at first, our resisters demoralized the invader army. We'd sneak in at night, attack with our hunting muskets, then disappear into the forests and hills. We won a few skirmishes, but losses were heavy. In the second year, our weapons rusted, and we ran short on ammunition. Many in our group lost the will to fight. Soon, only fifty-one remained. Next came the massacre in the Valley of Santa Maria. Fifty resisters died that day, as spears and arrows rained down on them from hundreds of warriors. The leader assigned me to remain behind and guard their wives and children. Now, this same group meets in my barn to talk of regaining our freedom. We have the will, but not the weapons or knowledge to engage in battle with this brutal enemy."

Timo shook his head. "Forgive me. I'm an old man, rambling on like this. Our troubles are not your burden to bear. You boys look tired and worn out, so please stay here tonight. My barn's out back." He pointed to a pile of blankets in a corner. "Each of you take one of these quilts and I'll get you settled for the evening. We'll continue our conversation in the morning."

The elderly Utopian led the rescuers to his barn and introduced them to the rest of his family. Patting a coal-black mule, he grinned and said, "In the old days before the invaders came, our island traded with the mainland to the north. We received livestock, like Galapagos here, in exchange for our tropical fruits and vegetables."

He winked and nodded toward the two cows in the adjacent stall. "Matilda and Emily are my milk cows. They'll leave you alone, other than a bit of mooing near dawn to wake you up. Sleep well, my friends." They thanked their host for his hospitality and watched as he strolled back to his tiny cottage.

The three rescuers plopped onto the bales of hay, exhausted but wide awake from the night's events. All except Jim talked eagerly about returning to Shell Beach. Ben was worried about his wife, Tilly, who had a rare form of bone cancer. The hospital was still running tests, so the man had a plateful of problems to deal with. JT ran a thriving business with his brother, John Phillip, fixing classic automobiles for wealthy clients.

Jim lived alone aboard a 42-foot cabin cruiser named *Rebecca* at the marina near the coast guard base. She was a vintage 1960s classic wooden hull motorboat, with curves like a woman, graceful as a ballerina underway. Her varnished woodwork sparkled in the sunlight. With the help of JT, he kept her diesel engine tuned like a Steinway piano.

As he nodded off, his mind painted a picture of his other Rebecca, his wife, and the love of his life. She had waist-length blond hair and sky-blue eyes. Warm, kind, and strong. Adored by all the kids at the local elementary school, where she worked in the front office. He taught her to sail, and she loved to take their small dinghy out by herself, challenging the ocean alone.

One year ago, everything in his world changed. It was late Friday afternoon when an inbound shrimp trawler reported an overturned sailboat about a mile off the inlet. Jim, Ben, and JT had duty together that day.

As the rescue boat pulled alongside the sailboat, the tanned left arm of a body, trapped beneath, floated to the surface. Jim recognized Rebecca's wedding ring right away, the one he'd hand-woven from tiny strands of silver wire into an intricate Turk's-head knot. In an instant, his life, like the dinghy, capsized into a bottomless black abyss.

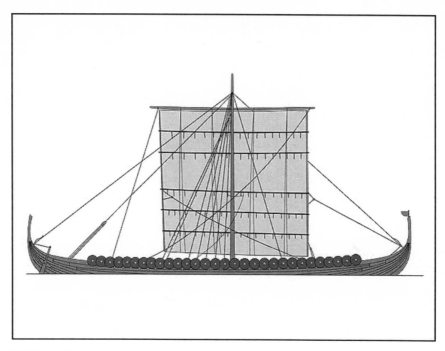

Viking Longship — Renowned for their seaworthiness and robust construction, longships were built from oak or pine, and could be rowed or sailed. Speed averaged 5 to 6 knots under oars, and 5 to 15 knots under sail. (Illustration from Wikipedia).

Chapter 7

Sunbeams streaked through the slats of the barn, dancing on Jim's face. He rolled over, rubbing the sleep from his eyes. Ben and JT were still asleep. He wanted to talk to Timo alone to discuss an idea which came to him during the night, so he grabbed his coat and walked up the path to the cottage.

The elder Utopian greeted Jim with a hug, invited him in, and motioned him to sit at the wooden table. Timo poured tea into clay mugs and handed one to his guest.

Jim thanked him and said, "Timo, there might be a way to give your resisters the edge to take back your island from these invaders. I own a powerboat, about the same size as the one tied up in your lagoon. My idea is to load her up with rifles, ammunition, books, and other supplies. I'll get underway, take her through the crescent, drop off the provisions, and return to my home in Shell Beach. So, what do you think?"

Timo's mouth dropped open. "Jim, that's the most generous offer I've ever had. If we had those guns and ammunition, we could make a stand. But it seems way too risky for you. I can't ask you to do this."

Squeezing the older man's arm, Jim said, "There are no guarantees, and it might be just me returning. Ben and JT will have to decide whether to take the risk. They have families, but I don't. My coast guard enlistment ends in a week. After that, I'm free. Those are my plans."

Timo shook Jim's hand, thanking him again for his generosity. "What time will you and your crew depart tonight, my friend?"

"Before midnight, Timo. We've been missing from the station for over a day. If we can find this crescent again, we should arrive back at our base tomorrow morning. So, according to the theory, that will be June 9, 2029?"

Timo nodded. "Correct, Jim, but remember, you must pass through the exact center of the black crescent, or you might end up in a different year or millennium."

Jim swallowed hard, his mind filled with scenes of growling dinosaurs, cave men with clubs chasing cave women, and erupting volcanoes spewing copious buckets of lava, like spaghetti sauce running over the sides of a boiling pot.

Timo added, "In less than thirty days, the crescent fades away for two more decades. There's no turning back. Wherever you are at that moment in time is where you stay for another twenty years. Before you go, I have something for you." He reached into a tiny footlocker at the side of his cot, pulled out a leather bag, and laid it on the hardwood tabletop.

"These will serve two purposes—to prove to others where you have been and to purchase the supplies we need to take back our island. Please accept this as a small token of my appreciation for what you and your fearless crew are doing. Go ahead, you may open the gift now."

Jim untied the leather drawstrings, shaking the bag's contents onto the table. Gold coins spilled out, glistening in the morning light. On one side, each coin showed Utopia de Paz stamped in intricate detail. The artwork was exquisite. On the back, the date, "Fourteen Hundred Sixty-Five," was stamped below an embossed cross superimposed over a profile of the hourglass-shaped island.

"Timo, these are priceless coins, and I appreciate your kindness, but don't you need these for your own livelihood?"

Shaking his head, Timo said with a smile, "Don't worry, my friend, these treasures have no value in my world. I keep them as a reminder of more peaceful times. Use what you need to buy us weapons, ammunition, and books. Bring me back what remains. I trust you, Jim, and your good crew, Ben and JT. You are risking your lives to help us."

Timo picked up a coin, turned it over in his hand and said, "These are solid gold from the mines in the Santa Maria mountains. Any expert can verify their value. They've been in my old footlocker for twenty years. It's about time they did more than gather dust. Now, let's put them to use."

Jim carefully replaced the treasure in the purse, tied the drawstrings tight, and tucked the bag into his cargo pants pocket. A knock on the door announced the two late sleepers had arrived. Timo welcomed the crew into his humble abode, poured fresh mugs of herbal tea, and served a tasty meal of scrambled eggs and cracked-wheat bread.

As they ate, Timo talked about the farm, his hobby as an amateur botanist, and more about the effects of the invasion on the Utopians.

"Before the Viking longships landed on these shores, our people lived over one-hundred years. It all changed a few months after the enemy arrived. They brought diseases. My beautiful wife, Magdalena, died of tuberculosis less than a year later. For the next ten years, I dedicated my life to the study of plants and flowers indigenous to this island. This led to the discovery of an elixir of such potency that it boosts the immune system against all disease. The tea you drink now contains these herbs. You must brew and consume the liquid within one hour of picking the Golden Spindle flower, which only grows here on Utopia."

As Timo told the story of his discovery of the magical tea, Big Ben asked questions about its effect on cancer, to which Timo replied, "Ben, the Utopians do not have the afflictions you describe. They live long, healthy lives. Those who had existing diseases must ingest the tea every day to remain free of illness. The caveat is like I described before; once you pick the flower, you must brew the petals right away and drink the liquid. It turns rancid if stored, so it will not keep past the short time window."

Ben nodded, grimacing, his mind churning as he thought about how the tea might help Tilly with her cancer. The three crewmen spent the rest of the day getting the boat ready to depart.

Near midnight, the rescuers waved goodbye to Timo, slipped the mooring lines, and entered the Gulf of Mexico. Jim pushed the throttles up to full speed and aimed the bow toward the last position of the black crescent, gateway to home and the 21st century.

Chapter 8

The rescue boat rolled from side to side like a drunken sailor in the choppy seas of the Gulf. Ben returned to the pilothouse after stowing the docking lines. "Wind's picking up, Skipper. We have a nasty gale headed our way."

Jim nodded, thankful for the thick thunderclouds covering the sky, which would help hide them from the Viking longships guarding the coast.

JT stepped into the cabin. "Both diesels are running smooth as a baby's bottom, Skip. Got a small oil leak in the starboard engine, but nothing to worry about."

"Thanks, JT. We'll monitor the oil pressure on our way home."

As they sped along, Jim thought back to when he and Timo talked alone in the cottage. After Rebecca died, he'd given up on life, wondering what he was going to do after he left the coast guard next week. The idea of going back to the mysterious island of Utopia was nuts, but the elder resistance leader's words touched his heart, gave him purpose, a reason to keep going.

Once they arrived back at Shell Beach, he'd tell Ben and JT about his plans. He would need JT's brother's help to buy rifles and ammunition. John Phillip served for ten years as a Navy Seal weapons and tactics instructor before being discharged because of partial blindness in his right eye. He was also an avid coin collector and he was friends with experts who worked in the industry.

"JT, relieve me on the wheel. I need to check our position." The young engineer slid into the helm seat, and Jim climbed down the ladder to the lower cabin. He plotted their location on the nautical chart and estimated the distance to the black crescent. They should sight the target on radar any time now.

He remembered Timo's warning to pass through the exact center. That would be a heck of a challenge in calm weather, but it might be impossible in a storm like this. Would they end up in an arena fighting Roman gladiators, in a Revolutionary War skirmish, or in a WWII sea battle dodging U-boats?

Jim shook his head to stay focused, then called up to the pilothouse. "Ben, got any contacts ahead of us painting on the scope?"

"Nothing showing up yet, Skipper. But, wait. Hold on. I see a long, narrow contact just over three miles dead ahead. The shape looks the same as it did the first time. Gotta be that crescent."

Jim dashed up the companionway to the radar system. Sure enough, the target appeared as a well-defined eyebrow shape, closing fast. Gigantic waves shoved the rescue craft to the right and left as they made their approach. Buckets of sea water lashed the windshield as the boat pitched up and down. Using the radar, Jim helped JT steer toward the center of the crescent.

When they closed to within two miles, the temperature plummeted like a snowball rolling off the face of a cliff. Sheets of freezing rain pummeled the vessel, rat-a-tat-tatting on the glass of the pilothouse windows. The shrieking wind battered the tiny ship as JT fought to keep her on course.

As before, the diesel engines took on a mind of their own, and no matter how hard Jim pulled back on the throttles, the boat refused to respond, speeding like a bullet toward the black barrier, looming in their path.

Ben shouted above the noise of the wind and pounding seas, "Skip, we lost radar power!"

Jim reset the electrical breaker, but nothing happened. As they entered the crescent, darkness closed in like a thick fog. The only sound came from the racing engines. How long did they have until the red-hot diesels burst apart, leaving the rescuers adrift inside the shadowy tunnel?

Chapter 9

Less than a minute passed before both engines sputtered and stopped. The thunderous noise of the storm sounded far away, echoing inside the cavernous tunnel. Light from the steering compass cast a reddish glow on the faces of the rescuers as they stared ahead into the endless blackness of the crescent. The boat sped along at breakneck speed, the magnetic force now in complete control.

Ben tapped Jim on the shoulder. "Skip, I see a light off the starboard bow. Faint, but it's there." Jim grabbed his binoculars and saw what appeared to be a candle flame flickering in the distance.

Seconds later, they shot out of the tunnel, drifting to a stop in a flat-calm sea. The three men stepped out onto the deck, gazing up at the giant canopy of twinkling stars. A gigantic yellow-orange moon peaked above the eastern horizon, and the placid Gulf waters filled the air with sweet saltiness.

Jim turned to his engineer and said, "Okay, JT, give me my engines so we can head for home." The young crewman answered with an informal salute and dashed back into the pilothouse. Within seconds, the diesels rumbled to life like a pair of playful lions.

"Engine oil pressure and water temp are normal, Skip. No harm done. Ready to rock."

The radar came back on, showing the profile of Florida's west coast fourteen miles away. Checking the chart one more time, Jim plotted a new compass course to Shell Beach inlet. He punched the blue night light on his wristwatch, noting it was 4:35 in the morning. They should make landfall in less than an hour.

He turned to Ben and said, "Okay guy, take the wheel, steer due east, run her up to full speed, and let's take her home."

By 5:30 a.m., the exhausted crew sighted the familiar short-long, white flashing light of the sea buoy. Thirty minutes later, they tied up in their slip. The base seemed deserted, but Jim figured it was too early for anyone to be up and about.

After telling Ben and JT to stay aboard and finish cleaning the boat, he stepped onto the dew-slick dock, hurrying down the sidewalk to the on-base bowling alley. There, he would find the answer to the burning question they all had; what month, day, and year had they arrived?

He held his breath as he rounded the corner, seeing the high-resolution LED screen outside. It featured announcements for upcoming events, and the current day and time. He waited for the display to cycle through to the date page. Bold, black letters against a white background announced, "Good Morning! Today is Saturday, June 9, 2029."

Jim felt a massive weight lifted off his shoulders. After losing power to the radar, he feared they would miss the middle of the crescent. Now he understood. The wall had a narrow tunnel at its exact center, one way in and out. No matter where you were as you approached, the magnetic force would pull you through the slender neck. This boosted his confidence for the return trip to Timo's island in his own cabin cruiser.

He jogged back to the boat to share the news with his crew. Ben and JT, now relieved and excited, were itching to step ashore, but Jim reminded them to wait until he checked in with the duty officer.

As the skipper entered the administrative office, Petty Officer Karen Stanley, the night duty watch stander, was at the coffee machine in her stocking feet. Karen was a young, slender, black woman with a perky personality and a generous smile. She turned around, her eyes widening with fright as she let out a squeal and dropped her ceramic mug onto the carpet.

"Oh my God, I'm seeing a ghost or the real Jim McGraw! Where on earth have you been? We've got half of the Florida Coast

Guard out looking for you guys!" Stanley gave Jim a hug and said, "Are you okay? Where's your crew? Where were you all this time?"

No one would believe the true story of the black crescent, landing on an island in the 19th century, or Viking invaders and a ragtag group of resisters, led by a man named Timo. So, the rescuers had concocted an imaginary tale to tell everyone they encountered.

"We're all fine, Karen. Both guys are down at the docks cleaning up the boat. Storm came up. Our radio fried, and we lost all communication with the base. Next, one of our engines died, so we anchored behind a barrier island. JT spent two days troubleshooting the problem, which turned out to be a clogged fuel line. Took a while to fix everything so we could get home, but here we are."

Jim asked about the vessel in distress the night they left. Stanley shook her head and said, "It was a hoax. Some bored live-at-home college kid getting his jollies, sending the CG on a wild goose chase. The feds tracked the signal to a beach bungalow in Pensacola. Caught him red-handed, making another false distress call. Can you believe it?"

"I'm glad it wasn't an actual case. Nasty weather that night. So, Karen, my crew's been on a diet of survival rations for the last few days. We're starved. What's on the breakfast menu?"

She laughed and said, "Nothing's changed. Same as usual. Cook's cuisine still rates one star in the Michelin Guide. Tell your crew to come on up for coffee and chow. I'll wake up Chief Higgins, so he can call off the search parties."

Jim thanked her and took off back to the docks. So, Higgins was the duty officer, a paper pusher, but an alright guy who respected the boat crews. He should swallow their story without a problem, but that left Warrant Officer Stansky, his immediate supervisor, and a different breed altogether.

The two men got along about as well as a cobra and a mongoose. When Jim first reported to the base, Stansky wanted to assign him to administrative duties because they were short on staff. But Jim was an expert sailor, having owned and lived aboard his own boat for years. He wanted to drive rescue boats, not sit at a desk answering incoming calls.

He submitted three requests to Stansky asking to be assigned as small-boat coxswain, but all were denied. Fed up, he took it to the next level, the base commander. That day, she ordered the warrant officer to add Jim's name to the skipper list. Afterward, Stansky looked for any opportunity to give him grief.

So, he wasn't out of the woods yet. Jim still had to convince his boss to grant him leave so he could return to Utopia with provisions for Timo and his band of resisters. And the time to pass through the black crescent was getting shorter by the minute.

Chapter 10

After drinking enough coffee to sink a battleship and devouring a plate of the cook's rubbery breakfast fare, the crew met with Chief Higgins to tell their story. The watch officer turned Ben and JT loose after grilling them for a half hour. Jim stayed behind, waiting for the interrogation with Stansky.

He patted his cargo pants pocket to make sure Timo's priceless purse of gold was still there. Earlier at breakfast, he told both crew members of his intentions to return to Utopia aboard his own boat. They were excited and, to Jim's surprise, volunteered right away to help find supplies and weapons for the trip.

The precious gold coinage got both men's attention right away as they picked up a sample of the glistening metal, turning it over and over in their hands.

JT grinned and spoke first. "Man, oh man, Skip, this would put John Phillip in coin heaven, for sure. Why don't you let me show him one of these gold pieces? His buddy experts could figure out what they're worth. What do you say, Skip? We could all meet at your boat tomorrow to talk more."

Ben nodded in agreement. "I've been thinking about Timo's tea every minute since we left the island, Skipper. The doctors are fresh out of ideas on how to beat Tilly's cancer. I believe what Timo said about how his special brew can cure any disease. One thing's for sure, If Tilly stays here, I believe she'll get worse and . . ." Ben stopped mid-sentence, swallowed hard and continued. "I don't want to lose her, Skip. But, she's not gonna believe the story coming from me, so I'll need your help to talk her into making the trip."

Jim gave each of the crew a coin to show to their loved ones. As Timo suggested, the gold might be the catalyst to convince others of the actual story. They all agreed to meet aboard the *Rebecca* on Sunday afternoon. Twenty minutes after Ben and JT departed, Warrant

Officer Stansky arrived, huffing and puffing like a locomotive. Jim figured he and the crew showing up on a Saturday must have interrupted Stansky's weekend barbecue.

After describing the events according to the concocted script, Jim handed Stansky his request for leave. He wanted to begin his vacation Monday morning and continue through the end of his current enlistment, just seven days away. There wasn't much Stansky could do, except rant and rave, which is exactly what happened.

"So, let me get this straight. You want me to grant you time off for the next week, McGraw? Are you crazy? We've had sixteen units out doing search patterns twenty-four hours a day. Now, you show up on a Saturday looking fit as a fiddle."

Jim reminded Stansky he had more than enough leave saved and that the base was now flush with experienced coxswains and boat crew. Stansky shook his head and dropped the leave-of-absence request on the pile of papers on his desk. "I'll shoot this up to the commander, but no guarantees." In Jim's case, that meant it had a better-than-average chance of approval. Stansky realized Jim would not hesitate to take this to the base commander if the belligerent officer failed to follow through.

Jim left Stansky's office and spent the rest of the day filling out paperwork on the incident. Of course, the story fit the one the crew agreed on. He finished around five o'clock in the afternoon, walking the mile and a half to his boat at the Shell Beach Marina.

Mick, the tall, burly, red-haired dockmaster, was shutting down the fuel pumps for the night. He greeted Jim with an enormous bear hug. "Well, look who's come back from the dead! Just saw your picture on the five o'clock news channel. They said you guys showed up out of nowhere. So, what happened?"

Jim recited the cover story to Mick, then walked down the docks to his cruising trawler. The *Rebecca's* sleek lines and clean decks spoke of a man who kept her shipshape and ready for sea. Everyone told him she was a 'show-stopper' and Jim had to agree.

Stepping aboard, Jim went below to open the hidden safe behind a false panel next to the rope locker. He buried the bag of coins under the ship's insurance papers, closed the heavy lid, and tapped a new combo into the keypad.

His thoughts wandered back to Ben's conversation. How would Tilly react when Ben showed up? Her husband takes off in the wee hours of the morning on a mayday rescue mission, and there was no sign of the boat or crew after two days of searching.

Same with JT and his brother John Phillip. Both of his close friends had their work cut out for them. They needed to convince their families of the actual story, not the fake one.

Opening the small, compact refrigerator in the galley, he grabbed a block of provolone cheese, popped open a can of Mediterranean sardines in olive oil, and sliced off a hunk of two-day-old sourdough bread. Two glasses of chilled California red wine helped him wind down from the stress.

After eating, Jim settled into the lower bunk in the cabin, reading the next chapter of a detective thriller. His eyelids drooped, and he dozed off, dreaming about a tropical island with lush green mountains and waterfalls tumbling down cliffs into a lagoon. Off the coast swam sea serpents, snake-like heads held high, tongues flickering, ready to devour those who tried to enter or escape.

Chapter 11

JT drove Ben to his small bungalow at the end of Port Walton Street, a few miles from the base. Ben's heart skipped a beat as they pulled into the gravel driveway. Where was Tilly's car? The home was dark except for the faint glimmer of the yellow porch light.

"Well, big guy, here we are. Looks like Tilly's out and about. She'll be home soon. You'll see. You are one lucky dude to have a woman like her!"

"No complaints, my friend. Thanks for the lift. Catch you tomorrow." Weary with fatigue, Ben climbed the steps, opened the screen door, and stepped inside. Switching on the light, the first thing that caught his eye was the sleeping bag on the couch next to the fireplace.

Maybe she was at the beach hanging out with their neighbors. He glanced at the clock above the mantle. Already 10:00 p.m.? Ben sat down to wait for Tilly, staring at the time as the hands rolled past 10:30. 11:00. 11:30.

She never stayed out this late. He and Tilly were what he called 'Benjamin Franklinites', early to bed, early to rise. They made this a habit. They had a secret routine they stuck to most days of the week. Up before sunrise; they'd work out with weights, kettlebells, and body-weight exercises. Next, they'd meditate and pray while walking hand in hand down to the fine white-sand beach, gazing up at the dawn sky, alive with shining stars and planets.

Before the sun peeked over the horizon, they'd return to their tiny home, toss together eggs, bacon, and English muffins for breakfast, sit out on the back patio, whispering as they ate, greeting the first light of the new day. Simple things like this made them happy.

Ben turned off all the lights except for the wall receptacle nightlights. He wondered if she'd gotten his voicemail messages, telling her he was safe and waiting at home. Why wasn't she returning his calls? He slapped his forehead. Now he remembered. Early last week, he'd asked her if she wanted to walk down to the beach and have a picnic this Saturday.

Tilly said she had to work the graveyard shift at the ER all weekend. She and her team would work nonstop all night, stitching up a drunk, a car wreck victim, saving a heroin addict, or treating a homeless veteran's infection. They faced challenges like this every day at the Shell Beach Hospital Emergency Room.

She should be home a few minutes after 5:00 a.m. He walked back to their bedroom, sat down, removed his shoes, and stretched out. He would give himself two hours of shut-eye before Tilly got home. Seconds after closing his eyes, he dozed off into a deep slumber.

Ben was a super light sleeper. Any sound would wake him, which drove him nuts on boats or ships until he adjusted. After a while, he discovered the sounds of the sea, the rumble of an engine, or the rocking of the boat helped him sleep through most anything.

Yet on land, he still jerked awake at the tiniest noise. A locomotive's shrill whistle, a mockingbird's bright song, a dog's anxious bark, or a child's playful giggle.

Sunday morning, a loud bang from the front of the house woke him. It took a few seconds for Ben to realize it was the screen door slamming against the frame. Glancing at the bedside table, the alarm clock's digital numbers glared back at him; 5:30 a.m. Tilly was home from work.

Ben rolled out of bed, pulled on his shirt, then walked down the hallway to the kitchen. Tilly had her back to him, dressed in her scrubs, sexy as ever. She laid her keys on the counter, set her purse down, turned around and the moment their eyes met, Ben smiled and said, "Hi Tilly, I've come home!"

Tilly's hand went to her mouth as she gasped. Her eyes rolled back as she fainted, falling forward right into Ben's arms, catching him totally by surprise. He picked her up, carried her over to the couch, and checked her vital signs to make sure she was okay.

Satisfied that Tilly was fine, he covered her with a blanket, then sat with her, holding her beautiful hands in his. He had been missing for over two days, but for Tilly, it must have been a lifetime. Now he shows up like a dark shadow in a graveyard? No wonder she passed out when he appeared out of nowhere. He gazed down at the woman he loved, her black curly shoulder-length hair splayed across the pillow, her mocha-colored skin and her slender body.

He whispered, "Tilly, if you can hear me, I've come back. We didn't die out there, and I'm no ghost. Same old Ben. When you wake up, I'll tell you all about an island surrounded by Viking ships and an elderly guy with a long white beard who lives in a cottage. He's got this tea and it can cure anything, and it will make you better. You rest for now, girl. You're gonna think I'm crazy when I tell you the story, but after you talk to Jim tomorrow, everything'll make sense."

He kissed her gently on the cheek, nestling his head next to her soft shoulder. Within the hour, Ben dozed off, holding Tilly's hand in his, content and at peace.

Chapter 12

Steam drifted off the marsh surface like ghostly fingers in the humid air. The awakening of another scorching hot day in the mosquito state of Louisiana. John Phillip woke up sweating bullets, his head filled with dreadful thoughts of his younger brother, JT, the kid he'd raised almost single-handed. What had happened to him?

A few days earlier, JT took off on a rescue mission and never came back. He remembered the call coming in at three o'clock in the morning, figuring it was bad news. There was something eerie about the sound of the ring-tone. It was a lieutenant named Fitzgerald, who said, "Mr. Tecumseh, I regret to inform you that your brother, Jared Thomas, and the rest of his boat crew, are missing. We have search units looking now, but so far, nothing's been found. We'll keep you posted."

Nothing hit him as hard as those words. He'd been like a father to JT from birth, his mother refusing to have anything to do with him. After she delivered Jared Tecumseh, she'd brought him home, dropped him off in a laundry basket at the front door, and rang the doorbell. John Phillip found his baby brother tired and hungry, crying in the cold. The news of his disappearance tore a hole in his heart, leaving him empty, pushing his sanity to the edge. Now, lack of sleep was wearing him down.

He rolled out of bed, realizing he had to move on with his life, one day at a time. Maybe today would be the day they'd find out something, because not knowing was worse than the worst news. He'd take a quick shower, then call the base again for the hundredth time. John Phillip stepped into the stall, turning on the water to the coldest setting, washing off the sweat.

Five minutes later he finished, grabbed a towel, his thoughts interrupted by the shrill ring of his cell coming from the bedroom. Now, who the heck would call at 5:00 a.m.? Dripping wet, he dashed down the hallway, picked up the cellphone, and heard a familiar voice on the other end.

"Hi bro, what's up, dude? How about I swing by your pad and pick you up? We'll grab breakfast at Al's Diner." JT figured he'd better say it in one shot before his older brother exploded. Which, of course, was what happened next.

John Phillip shouted into the phone. "You little pipsqueak! Where are you? Thought you were swimming with the sharks, what with you disappearing into thin air and all! Holy cow, Jared, half the dang coast guard's been looking for you clowns."

JT laughed and said, "Slow down, bro. Take a deep breath. We lost communications and our navigation equipment went down, and so did our engines. I'll explain more when I get to your place. I'm on the road now, so I'll be there before too long."

They signed off, and John Phillip felt all the tension of the last forty-eight hours wash away like surf breaking on a beach. He pumped both fists skyward, belting out an *Oorah* like his platoon used to do during his time as a Navy Seal. He couldn't wait to listen to the rest of JT's story. In less than an hour, his little brother arrived, grinning like a Cheshire cat. The brothers exchanged hugs and tears, neither holding back their emotions of love and relief for the miracle.

"Man, oh man, JT, you're back from the dead. What happened, guy? The base reported you missing in action and now you show up looking fit enough to fight? You gotta lot of explaining to do, little bro. Let's take your truck and go grab some grub and you can tell me all about it."

Al's served an excellent breakfast, and the brothers sat outside, filling up on eggs, ham and grits. JT told the tale from start to finish, leaving nothing out. He started with the distress call from the vessel *Caroline*, the encounter with the mysterious black crescent, and the island of Utopia. He finished with Timo's tale of the Viking invaders and how the islanders wanted to regain their freedom.

John Phillip listened intently, staring into his brother's eyes as he babbled on and on. Now, to most folks, a story like this might appear to be a fairy tale or something from a science fiction film. But John Phillip had raised JT to never, ever tell a lie. He didn't tolerate liars, and he could spot one a mile away. And what appeared in the brown eyes of his little brother was solid truth, with not a lick of falsehood included.

Not that he understood anything. He figured JT might have hit his head in the engine room. He'd heard about sailors having hallucinations out at sea, not from drugs, but from fatigue. But what happened next made him a believer, or, at least, added credibility to his brother's amazing tale.

"Look bro, I know you think I've gone nuts, but have you ever seen anything like this?" JT handed over one of the gold coins Jim gave each of the crew to show their families. John Phillip was an amateur coin collector with twenty years of experience, a member of numismatic clubs, and he had contacts with the biggest names in the industry. His personal collection included coinage from the early nineteenth century.

JT waited as his brother turned the coin over and over, checking out the intricate details of the embossed artwork on each side. "Wish I'd brought my magnifying glass, but I'd have to say it has all the makings of the real deal. Dated 1465? This may be worth more than my entire collection! Just so happens that a colleague of mine is in town. He's a pro dealer for museums in New York, London, Paris."

John Phillip whipped out his phone and speed dialed his buddy, asking if he could estimate the price of an unusual coin. He disconnected, nodded and said, "Let's beat feet and go see my friend Alistair Livingston. He's the one man I trust to know the true market value of something this rare."

Twenty minutes later, JT parked the truck outside a red brick shop on the edge of town. A white sign with gold lettering hanging above the door said: We Buy and Sell Gold Coins. He held his breath, crossed his fingers, and hoped the appraisal would be enough to convince his big brother he hadn't lost his marbles.

Chapter 13

Tilly opened her eyes as the aroma of fresh coffee filled the room. She sat up on the couch, and Ben handed her a mug of steaming brew. "Had quite the shock last night, girl. Passed out, fell right into my arms. You okay?"

Tilly said with excitement, "Now I am. Darling, thank God you're alive! When did they find you guys?"

"No one found us, Till, and what actually happened, well, you're gonna find what I tell you hard to believe. But, here goes . . ." He started with the distress call from the *Caroline*, passing through the tunnel called the black crescent, finding Timo's cottage, and the history of Utopia and its people.

Tilly stared at him, mouth open, eyes filled with disbelief. "Let me get this straight. My husband and his crew passed through a time warp, ended up in the nineteenth century on an island in the middle of the Gulf of Mexico? Add to that, one occupied by Viking invaders? Ben, no one's gonna believe this. They'll toss all of you in the loony bin!"

He handed Tilly one of Timo's coins, hoping this might boost her confidence in his story. She gazed at the shiny surface for a few seconds, shook her head, and passed it back to Ben. "I don't understand any of this, darling. Is this genuine gold? JT's brother is the coin expert, not me."

"Tilly, your tests. Have they come back yet?"

Her eyes fill with tears as she nodded and said, "Positive. It's spread to my lymph nodes. My doctor says they can slow it down, but he's doubtful they can stop the growth. They caught it too late, Ben."

Speechless, all Ben could do was hold her in his gigantic arms and rock her back and forth as tears streamed down his face, not knowing what else to do. In a choking voice, he said, "Tilly, my heart tells me this man Timo can help you. He's a botanist who spent years creating this herbal tea which gets rid of all diseases. The islanders are never sick and live for over one-hundred years. But you have to brew and drink the tea right after picking the flowers and herbs, which only grow on Utopia. That might sound crazy, but modern medicine isn't helping, and chemo is making you sicker. Jim's taking his own boat, going back to deliver supplies to our friend Timo. I was thinking about . . ."

Tilly interrupted Ben. "No way, darling, you aren't going back to this mysterious island. As much as I love Jim—and his wife and I were the best of friends. But, he's out of his mind for thinking of trying to find this place again. Darling, we have to pray my cancer will go into remission. What else can we do?"

Ben wasn't giving up. Western medicine didn't have the cure for Tilly's disease. They had given her a death sentence, no matter if her doctors hadn't told her yet. The hospital would run more tests, subject her to rounds of chemo until her hair fell out, and she withered away. His heart told him that Timo's elixir was the answer to his wife's survival, her last chance before death came knocking on the door.

"Jim asked us to meet him at his boat this afternoon. Everything I've said will be clearer when you talk with him. Till, I'm not making this stuff up. Never told a lie and I don't plan on starting now."

Tilly looked hard into his eyes, then smiled, touched his cheek, kissed him and said, "Ben, you're the most honest person I've ever met, and I don't know what to think right now. Okay, I'll listen to what Jim has to say. But darling, I don't want you going anywhere, not after almost losing you once."

Ben nodded, deciding not to pursue it further. She'd made up her mind for now, and he'd let Jim take it from here. He kissed his wife, picked her up in his arms, and walked toward their bedroom.

Tilly laughed. "Now, big man, what do you think you're going to do with your bride?"

He kicked the door closed with one foot and smiled. "Girl, we've got tons of time before we gotta leave. Let's do a little catching up!" Tilly giggled with delight as her husband turned off the lights.

Chapter 14

The morning temperature hit 85 degrees when the couple left their home. They hopped into Tilly's Toyota and drove to Shell Beach Marina. JT and John Phillip were already on Jim's boat when Ben and Tilly arrived.

Tilly ran up to Jim and JT, gave each a hug, and stood back, looking at them with a twinkle in her eye. "Well, look at you, the ghost sailors of the Gulf, back from another misty mission. This husband of mine tells me you all had an awesome adventure out there. I'd say you two have a lot of explaining to do."

She embraced JT's brother and said, "John Phillip and I have been keeping each other company on our cell phones while you guys were out exploring mystical islands."

"Right on, Tilly. When JT told me his tale, I thought he'd been bopped on the head. Now, I'm not so sure." He reached into his pocket and placed the precious coin on the table. "Have you seen the coins, Tilly?"

She nodded, reached into her purse, and set the shiny disk of gold next to the first. "Ben showed me this gold coin. I'm not sure how to handle all of this right now. I find it all scary and amazing at the same time."

John Phillip picked up the new coin, turned it over, smiled and said, "Holy cow, this one's stamped 1423. The one JT handed me was 1465. Tilly, these coins are original. Nothing like them exists anywhere. On the way here, we stopped to talk to a friend who's a rare coin expert. This guy's worked for museums in New York, London, and Paris, so he knows his stuff. He spent over an hour examining the coin JT gave me. He said they are the real deal, and estimates it would fetch a million dollars. Okay Jim, you've got the floor. Tell us your story."

Starting from the beginning, the skipper described their adventure, leaving nothing out. When finished, he told them about his plans to return with supplies for Timo and his resisters. He figured this was the moment to quell any lingering doubts. Picking up the bag, which had been resting at his feet, he unlaced the drawstrings and poured the contents into a pile. The twenty-eight remaining gold coins glittered in the sunlight.

Tilly and John Phillip gasped, their mouths open, staring at the precious metal worth thirty million dollars or more in the current market.

Jim broke the silence. "Our friend Timo entrusted this treasure to my safekeeping, asking me to use what I needed to purchase weapons, ammunition, medical supplies, and books to help them fight for their freedom. These invaders are direct descendants of the original Vikings, armed to the teeth with spears, swords, battle axes, and bows and arrows. Timo says they are fast and brutal. My idea is to purchase rifles, ammunition, books, and medical supplies with the gold, load my boat, run back to Timo's, drop everything off, and return here."

The ex-Navy Seal stared off into the distance for several seconds, then asked, "Jim, you have awesome intentions, but how are you going to find this black crescent again? You could end up facing dinosaurs instead of Vikings if you land in the wrong millennium."

He nodded and said, "I understand your concern, but I trust Timo's advice, and he says the black crescent should remain in place until next month. I have vacation time saved up and my enlistment ends next week. So, I'm free from here on out. John Phillip, I need your help to find at least thirty-five rifles and boxes of ammunition. Maybe throw in some books on tactics. And Tilly, if you could find a source to purchase medical supplies in bulk, including antibiotics? Nothing illegal, let's do this by the book."

Tilly asked, "How long do you think you'll be gone this time, Jim?"

"I figure the entire trip should take three to five days, no more."

The close friends sat in silence, each lost in their thoughts. John Phillip was the first to speak. "Okay, let me talk to a friend of mine. He knows how to avoid the government red tape when purchasing firearms. As far as the tactics part of it, I can help with that. I've done a lot of guerrilla warfare training and I've written a few handbooks on tactics. I'll include those in the boxes you take back with you. Dang, I miss working with folks one on one! Wish I was going with you. I'll get moving on this project first thing in the morning."

Tilly replied next. "Jim, I'll put a list together of medical equipment focused on treating battle wounds, fighting infection, surgical gear, and simple pamphlets on emergency first aid."

After everyone departed, Jim leaned against the rail, watching the brown pelicans perched on nearby pilings. He wondered about the sanity of what he was doing, hoping one or more of his friends might volunteer to come with him.

Doubt clouded his mind, wondering if he'd end up in another century, adrift on an empty sea, no land in sight, lost forever. He shook off the negative thoughts, determined now more than ever to find Utopia again. Timo and his tiny band of resisters were waiting for him to return, and he would not let them down.

Chapter 15

Monday morning, Jim got the surprise of his life when his cell showed text messages from Ben and JT. They would return with him to Utopia, along with Tilly and John Phillip. He'd given JT's older brother five more of the gold coins for his friend to look over. And, of course, they were just as valuable as the first.

Tilly had a full month's vacation time saved up at the hospital. Ben convinced her that Timo's magic elixir might be her last chance for survival. The doctors had already warned her there was nothing more they could do. What did she have to lose?

Jim called everyone to explain the risks one more time, but they'd made up their minds. If possible, he wanted to depart before the end of the week. He advised the crew to pack for a seven-day trip, although he expected to be gone only three days. Once they arrived, the beauty of the island might entice them to hang around longer. Extra time would also allow the rescuers to show Timo how to use the equipment.

John Phillip would arrange with his gun dealer to deliver the rifles and ammunition, and return to Shell Beach later in his own vehicle. Tilly would put together an advanced first aid and surgical kit. As an experienced ER nurse, she would ride along as the ship's medical officer and teach Timo the finer points of treating wounds and infection.

JT stayed with Jim on his cabin cruiser to inspect the mechanical and electrical systems for the upcoming mission. "Every time I work on your boat, I'm in heaven, Skip. You've kept her clean and pristine, but I'll triple-check everything before we take off."

Ben met up with Jim and JT later that afternoon. The boatyard workers hauled the *Rebecca* out of the water, put her up on blocks and left the three friends to their labors. They scraped the barnacles, sanded the bottom of the boat, and applied two coats of paint to protect her from marine growth.

Next, they inspected her engine shaft, propeller, and rudder, finishing up by washing the hull. By late afternoon, she sparkled in the sunlight like a brand-new boat. The boatyard would launch the *Rebecca* first thing in the morning.

All three showered at the marina, then strolled down the beach road to the Surf and Turf restaurant where Tilly would meet them that evening. While waiting outside for Tilly to arrive, JT called his brother to learn more about the status of the firearms.

"Got awesome news, little bro. My buddy Sam can get the guns and ammo delivered before the weekend. Let me talk to the skipper."

JT handed Jim the phone. The ex-Navy Seal explained his friend would ship thirty-five lever-action all-weather rifles, along with repair and cleaning kits, plus a variety of other arms and explosives. Jim asked for more details.

"The rifles are perfect for a newbie, Jim. They have a twenty-inch barrel, fire ten rounds, and weigh in at seven pounds. Weatherproof, so they're tough enough to hold up in rain or the salty dampness of the tropics. Shoots both 357 Magnum and 38 Special caliber ammo. Accurate out to about one-hundred yards. I'll pack a few cases of my custom-made incendiary kits and trip wires, field tested in combat and guaranteed to pack a wallop. I asked my buddy to add two dozen revolvers and combat knives for close quarters stuff. With training, Timo and his resisters can kick those Vikings back to where they came from."

"Excellent news, John Phillip. Thirty-five rifles will arm every man and woman in Timo's group. How about ammunition?"

"Never can have enough, Skipper. Several thousand rounds would not be too much if your vessel can handle the weight. I think you should stock up on cases of each caliber of ammunition.

Not a cozy feeling running out of ammo in the middle of a life-or-death fight.

Before they signed off, JT's brother asked, "One more thing, Skip. Timo's folks don't know beans about weapons or how to survive when outnumbered by a highly experienced enemy. If we have time, I can show them how to use and maintain the weapons, along with guerrilla warfare hit-and-run tactics I taught in the Navy."

Jim said, "That'd be awesome. I remember Timo telling me about a secluded valley near a waterfall, about four miles from his cottage."

John Phillip replied with enthusiasm. "Sounds like an ideal spot for a day or two of weapons training, Skipper. Plus, the noise of water pouring over a cliff will help drown out the gunfire. Okay, let's plan on it. I'll run copies of my *Battle Tactics Handbook* for your friend Timo."

For the first time, Jim could see the tide turning in favor of the ragtag band of Utopian resisters. He prayed the crew would feel the same way after they experienced the wild ride through the crescent and arrived at the mysterious island on the far side of the world.

Chapter 16

The *Rebecca* was back in the water the next morning, ready for her sea trial. The crew would check and double-check each mechanical system while underway to make sure she was fit for the upcoming mission. As they entered the warm, blue-green Gulf waters, Jim ran her up to maximum speed. The bow rose majestically as the boat sliced through the water like a graceful dolphin.

Sharp turns, emergency crash-stops, and backing drills completed her tests; all passed without a hitch. After two hours, not a soul aboard doubted the *Rebecca's* ability to complete her mission. They tied up to the fuel dock to top off her twin tanks. Jim's boat had a cruising range of about 1500 miles, so they had plenty of gas to get to Utopia and back to Shell Beach.

Tilly met the crew as they were tying up in the slip. She handed four heavy canvas bags of medical gear up to Ben and JT, stepped aboard, and went below to help Jim organize the supplies for the voyage.

"How did your sea trial go, Jim?"

"Like a charm, Tilly. The boat's running excellent. Depends on when the rest of our cargo arrives, but we may take off a few days earlier, if that works for you?"

"Yep, my vacation started today, so consider me part of your crew, Skipper. And, I don't mind doing the dirty work, so let me know what you need me to do." Jim thanked her for her help, and asked everyone to rest up for the trip. He would call them as soon as he had an update on the delivery of the weapons and ammo.

Early Wednesday afternoon, John Phillip called to say the delivery truck was on the way. The rescuers would meet the vehicle at Jim's small storage unit across the street. He didn't want marina snoops hanging around, which might happen if a truck parked on the pier, and they started loading long wooden boxes onto his boat. Instead, they'd wait until near midnight to move the arms to the *Rebecca*.

Near sunset, the truck arrived, and the crew offloaded the cargo into the storage space. Afterward, they returned to the cabin cruiser to rest until nightfall. Jim roused his crew from their naps thirty minutes before midnight, and they used carts to transfer the remaining crates to the vessel. By 2:00 a.m. Thursday morning, all supplies were aboard.

JT called his brother to check on his schedule. "John Phillip will be here late Friday morning, Skip. He's stocked up on tactical books and manuals. Says he'll bring his personal gear with him, so he's ready to leave when we are."

Jim asked the crew, "What do you guys think about taking off late Friday night?" Ben, Tilly, and JT all agreed. "Okay, everyone, get some rest. I'll call you as soon as John Phillip arrives, and we'll meet back here and go shopping for food and any last-minute supplies."

John Phillip met the rescuers before noon on Friday, and they all went grocery shopping together, followed by a tasty meal at the Shell Beach Waterside Cafe. They spent the rest of the afternoon loading final provisions and tying down everything for sea. By midnight, the *Rebecca* was stocked and ready for her journey, her crew eager to depart.

As the diesel rumbled to life, Jim stepped into the pilothouse, noticing a small picture taped above the console. Ben told him the day he left for the Coast Guard, his father handed him the miniature painting and said, "This will help guide you through the storms of life." Two weeks later, Ben's father passed away, but he never forgot those words.

In vivid colors of black, white, brown, gold, and red, the artist had created a masterpiece, showing a young sailor standing at the wooden wheel of a sailing ship on a storm-tossed sea, gazing into the distance. No longer in fear, but now with a look of confidence and determination.

For behind him stood The Christ, one hand resting on his left shoulder, and the other pointing the way to a harbor filled with calm seas and fair winds, just over the horizon.

Chapter 17

A few minutes past midnight, the five rescuers rounded the breakwater, and Jim increased speed, pointing the *Rebecca's* bow toward the last known position of the crescent. The Gulf greeted the crew with calm seas, light winds, and an umbrella of twinkling stars overhead.

To the south, a freighter steamed northwest, headed for the port of New Orleans. Further east, fishing trawlers crawled at a slow pace near the shore, their brightly lighted outriggers extending off each side—giant spider-like arms with nets attached, scooping shrimp from the sea.

Tilley handed mugs of steaming coffee to the crew. One thing she insisted on was taking over the galley. Jim happily surrendered that task to the talented amateur gourmet chef who could whip up a tasty meal on a limited budget. He and his wife spent many memorable evenings sampling Tilly's Spanish or Chinese cuisine.

Jim passed the helm to Ben and stood back, watching the experienced sailor drive his boat with ease, one huge hand atop the wheel, the other resting on the throttle, and a satisfying smile on his face. A man in his element, at peace in doing what he did best. "So, how long until we get to the black crescent, Skip?"

"Should be close to fourteen miles ahead, Ben. I figure we'll pick it up on radar by 2:00 a.m. at the latest." Jim recalled once again Timo's warning that the wall might shift position by up to two miles.

"She's one sweet driving boat, Skipper. Kinda reminds me of my dad's fishing trawler, the *Melissa,* named after my mother. Like my mom, you could rely on her in the worst weather. She got us through tough times more than once."

Jim concentrated on the radar picture, figuring they were still too far away for a signal to ping off the crescent. His stomach churned, hoping the eyebrow shape would appear soon.

John Phillip asked to steer the boat, and Jim agreed, sending Ben up to the bow to scan the horizon. A few minutes later, he pointed to the right, turned and shouted, "Skipper, we've gotta contact, about ten degrees to starboard."

Jim joined Ben at the bow, straining his eyes through the binoculars, just able to make out a faint, black line, rising like a shadowy wall from the sea. He signaled for John Phillip to slow down as he hurried back to check the radar. No targets painted on the scope. Without warning, the power shut down to all their navigation equipment.

The faint glow of the red emergency lights illuminated the cabin. Next, the engine sputtered and died, and like the first time, the mysterious magnetic field took total control of the *Rebecca*, pulling her at breakneck speed toward the apparition ahead.

John Phillip broke the silence; his voice was taut with tension. "I don't like this, Skipper. Are you sure we won't end up in outer space? Can you stop the boat until daylight so we can see what we're dealing with?" Tilly had climbed up the ladder from the galley and was staring in horror at the wall, one hand clasped over her mouth.

Jim said with as much confidence as he could muster, "Look, you guys, like we talked about, this is exactly what happened before. Timo called this a lateral force of magnetism, which pulls you from one side to another. We should be through this in a few minutes, so hang in there." They both nodded, trying to stay calm in a situation beyond explanation.

Jim's mind filled with doubt, wondering about his decision to ask his friends to accompany him back to Utopia. What was he thinking? Sure, they'd volunteered, but their welfare rested on his shoulders. His eyes caught the glimmer of a soft blue light surrounding Ben's picture taped to the console. Mesmerized, he stared at the sailor clutching the wheel, being guided through the fearful sea storm. At that moment, calm came over him, knowing they were not alone, not by a long shot.

JT returned from the engine room, his headband light casting a reddish-orange glow. Wiping his hands on an oily rag, he said, "Temperature out there's dropping like a rock, Skip. Your engine's okay, but stuck in neutral. Nothing I can do until we pass through the tunnel to the other side."

Jim nodded to JT as the blackness surrounded the tiny vessel. He told everyone to hold on tight. Three minutes later, they shot out of the dark tunnel, drifting to a stop, rolling with a graceful motion in the calm swell. A warm breeze wafted through the open windows of the pilothouse, and the dazzling night sky brightened the sea surface as before. The electrical power came on with a reassuring hum. JT inspected the engine, giving Jim a thumbs-up. The skipper punched the start button, and the *Rebecca's* diesel fired up without hesitation.

"Okay, Big Ben, jump on the helm and run her up to maximum speed. Steer a course to the north. We should pick up Utopia anytime now."

As the boat turned, Jim stepped out into the humid night to join the others. Tilly and John Phillip stood at the rail, mouths open, gazing in wonder at the constellations and full moon, which appeared close enough to touch. He saw a sliver of confidence in their faces. This was only the first step in their mission of mercy. They still had to find Timo's lagoon and avoid the enemy longships as they approached the island.

Chapter 18

The outline of Utopia showed up on the radar at about six miles, and Jim took the wheel, sending Ben with his eagle-eyes up to the bow as lookout. He turned the cruising boat onto her new compass course, heading toward the eastern side of the island.

Soon after they changed course, Ben shouted back to the pilothouse as he pointed to the left. "Skipper, looks like one of those Viking ships is under oars, headed south, about four miles away. Just picking up their stern."

Jim acknowledged Ben's report, wondering why a ship would be underway in the middle of the night in winds which were too light to fill her sails. Where were they headed? Why not wait until daylight and a fresh breeze? He'd ask Timo once they landed.

He stopped the *Rebecca*, holding her position until the longship was out of sight, then passed the wheel to Ben. Twenty minutes later, the narrow opening to Timo's lagoon appeared between the lofty dunes of white sand and bent palm trees. Jim joined John Phillip and JT on the bow, all armed with rifles, taking no chances in a land occupied by hostile invaders.

Tilly stood by the depth sounder, shouting out the depths as they crept toward the lagoon. "Twenty feet. Fourteen feet. Ten feet. Six feet. Holding steady at six feet, Jim."

They moored with a stern anchor and two lines tied to tree trunks ashore to hold the bow in place. Jim signaled for Ben to shut down the engine. All became quiet except for the gentle rustle of the wind through the palm fronds, the chirp of night birds, and the song of cicadas from the dense, tropical forest.

As the crew gathered on the narrow strip of white-sand beach, they heard twigs snapping, coming from the interior of the dark foliage. The rescuers took cover behind the trees, aiming their weapons in that direction. A white, ghost-like figure entered the clearing, the shape turned, and right away Jim recognized his old friend.

Timo was dressed in a knee-length white robe, billowing in the soft breeze, a nightcap atop his head. And, as always, his Meerschaum pipe was tucked into one corner of his mouth.

He greeted Jim and his crew with a hearty laugh and said, "Well, hello, hello my friends! You made it back, Jim. And, there are more folks with you than when you left. Welcome to my home, all of you!"

Jim, Ben, and JT gave the elder resistance leader warm hugs, then introduced him to Tilly and John Phillip. Timo invited the weary rescuers to follow him to his cottage. A lazy plume of smoke rose from the stone chimney. Timo opened the door, waving his guests inside. The delicious aroma of fresh-picked vegetables and sourdough bread made their mouths water. Timo insisted they join him for dinner.

As they filled plates and bowls, he informed them the date was June 16th, but the actual time was seven o'clock in the evening. So, the rescuers had landed on the island on the correct date, but a few hours earlier. Overall, it was a rousing success, and they all breathed easier, congratulating one another for a safe journey. Jim had reminded the crew beforehand about Timo's insistence on reciting the 23rd Psalm before meals, so they took part in their host's pre-meal ritual.

The crew dug into the delicious meal and Timo asked, "So, how was your trip, Jim?"

"We had an excellent journey. We found the black crescent within two miles of the original position. As we approached your island, we sighted a Viking ship headed to the southeast. No wind tonight, so they were under oars."

Timo nodded. "Ah yes, one of their supply ships. They are returning to their home port to load up with fresh provisions and new warriors to relieve those who have been here. I do not know the name or location of this place, only that it lies a short distance to the south of Utopia. They always return in two to three days."

Jim said, "If you can destroy those ships, you could cut off their supply route, turning the tide in your favor. Without a steady stream of men and provisions, these invaders can't keep going."

John Philip added, "The skipper's got a point, Timo. We've brought 21st century weapons and ammunition for you, modern stuff that's far superior to anything the enemy possesses. With some training, you and your group could take back your island. I can help with that."

Jim listened to the passion in the ex-Navy Seal's voice, remembering how JT told him his brother often talked about using his skills again as a civilian instructor for the Navy. But life had gotten in the way. Had the elder resistance leader lit a spark of excitement?

"Oh, and Timo, before I forget," said Jim, pulling out the bag of gold coins from his knapsack and handing it to their host. "Here's the rest of your gold. A single coin was more than enough."

Timo lit his pipe and said, "Thank you, Jim, and God bless each of you for coming here. Our resisters meet tomorrow night in my barn. However, there is something I must tell you. We could have a collaborator in our group. A young woman named Catherine was seen talking to an invader several times this week. If she has betrayed us, you may all be in danger."

Chapter 19

The five rescuers sat in stunned silence for several seconds until Tilly spoke with calm confidence. "Timo, what if Catherine and this young man are in love? She may not have told him anything about your group. I believe if she wanted to betray you, she'd find a hiding place out of sight to carry on her affair. Sounds to me like she's naïve, not thinking straight, and so infatuated with her lover, she's not considering the consequences. I think you should ask her to come to your meeting and tell her side of the story."

Jim added, "Tilly's right, Timo. If Catherine told the enemy about your resisters, you'd all be in jail. I suggest you wait until right before your meeting. Send two of your members to her cottage to escort her here. Put her in front of your people and find out what's going on."

"Both of you make excellent points," said Timo as he tamped a new plug into his pipe. "Catherine lives a mile and a half north of here. I'll assign two men to accompany her to our meeting tomorrow evening. Thank you for your insight, Tilly. We will listen to what she says before we decide what to do."

The crew helped Timo wash the dinner dishes, grabbed their knapsacks and walked to the barn to bed down for the night. They would offload the boat tomorrow morning and John Phillip was eager to check out the valley near the waterfall as a possible training sight.

Ben and Tilly climbed the ladder to the loft, while the other three took up their old spots next to Timo's mule and cows.

The moment Jim's head hit the soft hay pillow, the nightmares began. A massive dragon ship sailed at full speed toward his cabin cruiser. Round, colorful shields lined each side, and heavily armed men glared back at them with hate-filled eyes. The enemy vessel crashed into his boat, and the impact tossed the rescuers to the deck. The Vikings poured aboard like an army of ants, their battle axes swirling over their heads, swords slashing down, penetrating flesh and bone . . .

"Wake up, Skip. Skipper, wake up!" Jim opened his sleep-filled eyes, seeing JT hovering over him. "Must've been a doozy of a dream. Are you okay?"

Jim shook his head and yawned. "Yep, JT, all's good. You guys sleep alright?"

The youthful engineer laughed and said, "Out like a light. I wanted to break out the duct tape for John Phillip. He's like a dang chainsaw when he starts snoring. So, Skip, you want to move the weapons and ammo ashore first thing this morning?"

Jim replied, "Sounds like a plan, JT. Right after breakfast, we'll offload the boat." Timo had shown him a hidden cutout in the floorboards behind the barn. Stone steps descended to an underground shed where the elder resistance leader kept emergency supplies of food and water. Even if the invaders burned his cottage to the ground, his cellar would survive.

The rescuers met Timo for breakfast, then transported the arms and ammunition crates to the underground storage space. John Phillip unboxed the rifles, showing everyone how to clean and check the parts.

Timo and John Phillip left at noon to see the training area four miles inland, near the waterfall. While waiting for them to return, Jim, Ben, Tilly, and JT took turns guarding the *Rebecca*. Others, who were not on guard duty, rested up from the trip.

John Phillip returned from his excursion, excited to share the news. "We have a perfect spot for training, Skip. One of the biggest waterfalls I've ever seen. Reminds me of those pictures from Hawaii. Must be a hundred-foot drop to the stream below. Thunderous! I fired off a few rounds, and the falls drowned out the sound."

The light sparkled in his eyes as he spoke, which filled Jim with hope. Since their arrival, he'd noticed the same excitement in the rest of the crew. Being around Timo was like being in the presence of a mystic. His magnetic personality was mesmerizing, his words resonating with wisdom, warmth, and compassion.

But now, their immediate plans depended on what happened at the resister meeting tonight. If Catherine had collaborated with the enemy, they would need to leave right away. He hurried down to his boat, eager to inspect her one last time to make sure she was ready to get underway at a moment's notice.

Chapter 20

As darkness fell, a horned owl hooted from its perch deep within the forest. A full moon peeked from behind thick clouds as Timo's resistance group arrived by foot or mule and buggy. The five rescuers, armed with rifles, took positions to avoid detection. Jim and JT crouched behind a fallen coconut palm tree next to the front of the barn. Ben and Tilly guarded the boat in the lagoon, and John Phillip hid in the tall grass half a mile to the west, guarding the roadside approach to Timo's cottage.

Jim counted thirty villagers inside, some young, most middle-aged, and a few elders. Lanterns flickered as the group aired their concerns about a potential traitor in their midst. Timo's voice rose above the chatter. "She'll be here soon, and we'll ask her to explain her actions. Until then, she's innocent. Keep that in mind, all of you. Don't judge her until we have the facts."

Two of Timo's men would escort Catherine to the meeting. But they were already thirty minutes late. Jim conjured up a list of reasons. Had the woman found out Timo suspected her of treason and escaped to warn her Viking friend? Were the invaders on the way?

JT tapped Jim on the shoulder, pointing to a faint light bobbing up and down on the western approach road. Squinting through his binoculars, he sighted John Phillip jogging up the path at a fast pace. He met the ex-Navy Seal in the clearing.

"Something's not right, Skip. We've got four folks headed this way on foot. They're not in any rush, but it's hard to make out who they are. Black as tar tonight, except for that lantern they're carrying. Those two escorts and the lady make three, so why am I counting *four* people?"

"Okay, John Phillip. You and I will take a position on each side of the road. As they pass, we'll get a better look."

Silhouettes took on human form as the party approached. Two resisters, their muskets at the ready, walked behind a man and woman who had their hands tied behind their backs. The male prisoner had long blond hair and a thick beard. As they passed, the two rescuers fell in behind the group, glancing back to check for anyone approaching in the distance.

The two guards and their prisoners disappeared inside the barn. John Phillip took position outside of the door to listen to the interrogation. Jim stayed near the road to scan for invaders coming from the west.

Another hour passed before JT's brother jogged over to Jim and said, "We lucked out, Skip. Timo's two men burst through Catherine's cottage door and found the two at the table, eating dinner. The blond invader offered no resistance, and Catherine fainted, which was why they were late. They're still grilling Catherine and her boyfriend, so that's where it stands."

The hours trickled by as the questioning proceeded. Midnight came and went. A few minutes past 2:00 a.m., the meeting ended, the door swung open, and the weary resisters wandered outside, said their goodbyes, and departed.

After everyone left, Timo waved the rescuers over to the barn to tell them what happened. "Thank you all for your patience. Tilly, you were right, this is nothing more than a love affair. He goes by the name of Fredrick, and I find him to be a pleasant and intelligent young man. Fredrick's mother died in childbirth, so the invaders raised him, but he is Utopian by birth. No Viking blood flows through his veins. He is a ship's sailmaker by trade, not a warrior, but he hates being forced to live and work alongside those he despises. His dream is to marry Catherine one day and raise his children in peace, without fear. He leaves tomorrow on the ship to return to Thormanta, the Viking seaport, less than a day's sail from here. Fredrick has volunteered to record the courses steered on the journey and to tell us everything he learns once he returns."

Jim was elated, but wanted to know more about the island. "So, Timo, did Fredrick describe why the ships travel back and forth between the two islands? Your island has plenty of fertile ground for farming or growing tropical fruits and vegetables, and more than enough fresh water."

"Indeed, we do, Jim, but Fredrick says they use the forest on Thormanta, filled with gigantic oak trees, to build and repair their fleet of ships. Here in Utopia, our trees are much too small for shipbuilding. The warriors who return home for a break also tend their farms, growing hemp, wheat, and barley. Some raise sheep, cattle, and other livestock, acquired when they plundered the seacoast towns on the mainland to the north. Now, these towns have fortified their defenses, so the raiders steal from us instead. Before the invasion, Utopians traded with the merchants on the mainland. After we regain our freedom, the trade routes will reopen again, and our economy will flourish."

Jim finally understood the rest of the story. If they could locate and destroy the enemy base, Timo and his resisters could take back their occupied nation. Now came the tough decision for the rescuers; stay a few more days or head back to Shell Beach?

THE DRAGON'S LAIR

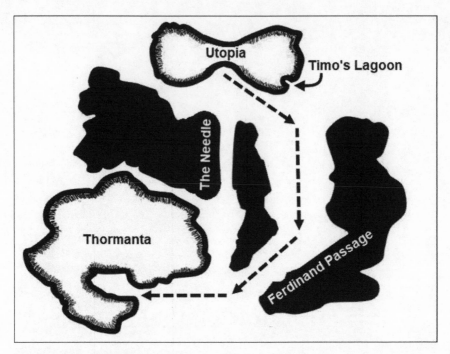

Viking Ship Sailing Routes — Dashed arrows are the four sailing courses the longships use on the journey from Utopia to Thormanta. Ships must sail these courses to avoid grounding on the dangerous coral reefs (solid black shaded areas).

Chapter 21

Late the next evening, the seaport of Utopia was a beehive of activity. Fredrick stacked bags onto the *Tristan,* a fifty-foot Viking longship scheduled to depart in one hour. The ship's captain, Ericson, a huge, ruddy faced-man with black hair and a grayish beard tied in braids, ordered more ballast stones to correct the tilt of the ship.

"She leans to the left, Fredrick. Add more weight to starboard until her mast points straight up toward Valhalla," he said, pointing skyward. "And hurry. I want to leave while we still have moonlight to help us navigate through the Ferdinand Passage."

Fredrick, being the senior sailor, directed his men to carry heavy stones aboard and place them beneath the floorboards. As they sweated in the humid air, the warriors who would sail back with them stood on the pier, talking with excitement about returning home. Earlier, Fredrick asked Erickson to allow him to man an oar closer to the stern. This would be the perfect spot to watch the ship's compass and hourglass, so he could memorize the courses and times. The captain granted his request without hesitation.

They finished provisioning the ship, and the warriors stepped aboard and took their seats. Laughter and lighthearted banter filled the night air. These men looked forward to a rest from their duties, and talked about drinking, being with women, and working their farms.

As Fredrick sat at his oar, he thought back to his last conversation with Catherine, remembering her reaching out with one hand to touch his heart. "Come back to me, Fredrick. I'm with you every moment, here in your heart. I will pray each hour for your safe return."

A shout from the pier woke him from his daydream as the crew cast off the final docking line and the ship drifted free. The captain ordered the men to dig their oars into the water as he swung the wooden tiller to one side, pointing the dragon-head bow toward the open sea.

As he bent his back to pull on the oar, Fredrick imagined what a life of freedom might feel like. In his mind, he and Catherine lived in her cottage next to the crystal-clear brook running behind the home. Their children—one, a brown-haired boy and the other, a girl with curly, blond hair—chased one another 'round and 'round. They swam in the brook, caught fish together, laughed and played, happy and free. He wanted that life to become a reality. But first, he must prove his loyalty to Timo and his brave band of resisters.

The bellowing voice of the captain interrupted his thoughts. "Fredrick, pay attention. No time for daydreaming. We shape our courses to sail around the shoals. Pull your load or I'll put you back in your old spot near the bow and let the motion of the boat and sea spray keep you awake!"

He nodded, pulling back hard on the oar as the ship sped over the calm ocean. They had hoisted the square white sail, but it slatted back and forth from the lack of wind. Fredrick kept his eye on the compass and hourglass, memorizing courses and times on each course. Hours later, the glimmer of the horizon appeared as the sun's morning rays illuminated the boundary between sea and sky.

Three more turns of the hourglass passed before he sighted the island of Thormanta, rising from the sea like the back of a gigantic whale. A few hours later, the *Tristan* sailed into the harbor. After tying up to the dock, Ericson said, "Fredrick, you are the senior sailor aboard, so I place you in charge of loading my ship. Remove the old supplies and stock up with fresh provisions. We sail for Utopia at first light. Let me know when you complete the task."

Fredrick nodded, then hoisted a heavy spool of rope onto his shoulder. He strolled down the pier to the wooden storage shed at the end. Alone now, he tossed the coil on top of the rest of the pile and hurried over to the table in the corner. A quill pen and ink bottle rested next to the leather-bound logbook which was used to keep track of supplies.

On the trip over, Fredrick composed a secret code to use in a love poem, or ode, to Catherine. He tore a page from the back of the journal, jotting down each line, inserting the encrypted code of the course directions and times into the poem.

Moments after he finished, a booming baritone voice startled him. "Fredrick! What are you doing?" Ericson stood at the doorway, glaring back at him with both hands planted on his hips. "Why is it taking you so long to record the supplies in the ledger?"

"Just finishing the journal entry now, Captain," he said, as he slipped the still wet paper under a loose plank on the right side of the desk. He closed the logbook as Ericson approached.

The captain clapped one powerful hand on Fredrick's shoulder and said, "Get a move on. You do not appear to be as attentive as before. Whatever's on your mind, you better put it to rest. Come, we have work to do."

Fredrick nodded, hurrying back to the longship, hoping he would have time to return to the storage shed and retrieve the priceless document before it was discovered by someone else.

Chapter 22

Timo asked the resisters to meet at his barn early the next afternoon and introduced them to Jim and the rescuers. As expected, their eyes filled with fear and distrust until John Phillip broke out the rifles and ammunition. Jaws dropped as the men and women gazed upon what appeared to be weapons from a science fiction novel. The future had arrived on the island of Utopia for this rag-tag band of revolutionaries.

The men gathered to touch the firearms and remark on their beauty and construction. After passing out ammunition, John Phillip led the group through the hidden path in the forest to the training grounds next to the towering waterfall.

Tilly and Timo would stay behind with Catherine. Timo still had doubts about allowing her to train with the others. Tilly offered to get closer to Catherine to uncover any threats to the resisters. So far, she'd found her to be honest and focused on her future with Fredrick.

As the rescuers approached the falls, their ears filled with the thunder of the water cascading into the stream at the bottom. The waterfall lay between the lush green hills of the Santa Maria Valley, with red and yellow flowers dotting the landscape, descending to the flat plain below. Now it was breathtaking in its peaceful beauty; not so long ago, this spot was the site of the bloodiest battle in Utopian history.

Jim, Ben, and JT spread out along the perimeter of the training site to guard for threats from the south. John Phillip passed out bags for targets, directing the group to fill them with dirt, placing them fifty feet away, staggered at ten-foot intervals. They practiced firing from standing, squatting and prone positions.

Next came the blindfold drill. The ex-Navy Seal handed out a long strip of cloth to be tied as a blindfold around each person's head. Everyone had to learn how to load and unload their weapons by feeling alone. If they had to fight in the dark, this single skill might save their lives. After a ten-minute break to eat some high energy food and drink water, they continued their training.

Blisters and bloody fingers didn't faze the resisters as they fired round after round into the dirt-filled targets. By late afternoon, half the men and women were shooting with more accuracy; the holes in each bag were getting closer together.

They moved on to emergency battlefield first aid. John Phillip showed how to control bleeding, pick up an injured comrade in a firefighter's carry, and how to create a makeshift stretcher from blankets and branches. Training ended close to sunset.

Before marching back, John Phillip gathered the group and said, "You have the weapons to win; now you need to learn tactics. Remember this: If a single Viking warrior gets wounded or dies, it will not have as much impact as if one of you becomes a casualty. I will teach you how to attack the invaders before they realize what happened. Confuse the enemy, and they panic, which leads to mistakes. Hit them hard, fast, and disappear before they can react."

After arriving back at Timo's cottage, John Phillip reminded the weary but excited resisters to stick to their normal routines at home to avoid suspicion. They would meet again in the morning to continue with their training.

Jim held a quick meeting with the rescuers to talk about extending their stay on Utopia for a few more days. All were ready to stay longer, having become closer to the men and women resisters during their short time on the island. Jim pointed out that they had two weeks left before the black crescent faded away, but even that sobering thought failed to dampen their enthusiasm.

The team broke up, and Big Ben pulled Jim aside. "Skipper, Timo's herbal tea is already helping Tilly. She slept through the night for the first time in over a month. She usually wakes up with searing pain in her head and joints. It keeps her awake for hours. Last night was like a miracle from God. Timo says this tea of his works right away, but you have to drink it every day. Taking it back to Shell Beach with us won't work. I don't know what to do right now. My father always said pray when you run out of ideas, so that's what I'm doing. Just wanted to keep you posted, Skipper."

Jim smiled and said, "Ben, excellent news about Tilly. This place has potential, but they have a long way to go to take back their island. It won't be a simple life if you remain here, but the Utopians are friendly people who care deeply for one another. They've treated us as if we were neighbors and a part of their community. You and Tilly won't be alone. Whatever you decide, I wish you the best."

After dinner, the rescuers talked about the next day's training. John Phillip said, "Timo, your folks have the will, which is half the battle. We start with tactics in the morning. Tomorrow's training will be tougher than today. I'm not gonna let up on them. You think they can handle it?"

Timo lit his pipe and said, "They realize the risks, and I've talked to them about the hard work it will take to learn to fight. They will perform their duties. Not one of my resisters complained today, which makes me proud, so proud. Now, I can only hope they continue with their determination. I believe they realize they are the ones who will change history. You, my friends, are showing us the door, but we must choose to take that final step over the threshold."

Everyone sitting at the table knew it would take a miracle to turn this ragged band of neophytes into men and women tough enough to face a brutal and battle-hardened enemy. Tomorrow, Fredrick would return from Thormanta with the most vital piece of the puzzle the resisters needed to win back their freedom.

Chapter 23

Fredrick crouched behind the wagon with eyes locked on the storage building across the street, waiting and watching for the men inside to depart. He sweated in the humid morning air, his nerves frayed, heart thundering in his chest. If he didn't return to the *Tristan* soon, Ericson would come looking for him. Minutes passed before the three men left, each carrying heavy rope coils, headed for the docks.

As soon as they were out of sight, he jogged over to the shed, made his way back to the log table, lifted the loose board, and pulled out the paper. Fredrick sighed with relief when he noticed that the ink had not smeared. Rolling the priceless document over a thin wooden dowel, he pushed it deep down into his leather boot.

Should he thank this mystical God whom Catherine talked about for his good fortune? After listening to her, he questioned the teachings of his youth. Were the priests wrong? Were there no gods of the sea, of love, of war? Could those be myths?

Fredrick grabbed three more coils of line, stepped out onto the road, and strolled down to the pier where men were loading the longship for her trip back to Utopia.

Stacks of weapons and supplies lined the wharf from one end to the other. Warriors and sailors stood shoulder to shoulder, passing the heavy brown canvas bags of provisions from one man to another down the line to the deck of the ship.

As he joined in with the others, his mind wandered back to the poem to Catherine. The first four lines contained the secret code of directions: *Smiling Eyes* = Southeast; *Sails* = South; *Soul Wanders* = Southwest; *Whispered* = West.

Dots at the end of a line containing one of these code words or phrases showed the number of hours to sail on each course.

Ode to Catherine

The light of your *Smiling Eyes*, like a beacon . .
fills my *Sails* and my heart with fair winds . . .
my *Soul Wanders* back to the last morning . .
before I departed, you *Whispered* a prayer . .
reminding me of the comfort of your embrace
and the love which awaits me when I return
to my fair lady, with her beauty and her grace

(The decoded first four lines are: Southeast for two hours; South
for three hours; Southwest for two hours; West for two hours).

Fredrick took his seat at the oar near the stern. The crew cast
off the docking lines, and the vessel moved out into the channel.
Sunlight danced on the waves in shades of red and yellow. An oily
swell rolled beneath the keel of the longship as a fresh breeze filled
her sail, pushing the hull with ease through the warm ocean water.

But to the east, the cloud-filled sky appeared reddish and
threatening. The *Tristan's* captain ignored the warning from Aegir, god
of the sea, unaware he was leading his ship and her crew into the jaws
of a raging storm.

Chapter 24

Hard, driving rain fell onto the resisters as they fired multiple rounds into their targets, jumping up from their squat position to move twenty-five yards to the right. Jim, John Phillip, Ben and JT worked with small groups to concentrate on speed and accuracy. As they practiced, Jim's mind wandered back to Fredrick.

They had to be taking it on the chin on the return voyage to Utopia. Storm-force winds and short, steep waves in the Gulf would challenge any ship, no matter the competence of her sailing crew. He prayed for Fredrick's safe return with the information gathered from the journey.

After another exhausting day of training, the weary rescuers made their way back to Timo's cottage. Tilly greeted them at the doorway and drew Jim aside. "Fredrick's ship is missing, Skipper. He told Catherine they would arrive by noon today, but so far, no ships have sailed into port. She's terrified that something has happened."

Jim asked, "Has anyone checked the harbor since this morning?"

Tilly nodded and said, "Yes, one of Timo's resisters named Thomas lives near the beach, so he can see any ship sailing in or out."

"Give them a chance, Tilly. I figure they're dealing with a full-blown gale right now, with howling winds and towering waves. If I were in this weather in my boat, I'd turn her up into the wind and seas and hold position until it passed. The storm will be gone before much longer. Let's wait until tomorrow morning."

Tilly thanked Jim for his words of encouragement, then left for Catherine's cottage to stay with her through the night.

The other rescuers cleaned and oiled their weapons and stowed them in the barn. Timo returned from a brief trip to the home of one of his resisters. He filled mugs with tea, passing them to each of the tired crew.

As he tamped a fresh plug of tobacco into his pipe, he said, "I just talked to my neighbor Carl, who serves as a blacksmith in town. He's listened to the warriors talking about their annual holiday celebration back on their home island. Most of the ships will sail from Utopia to Thormanta, including those which guard the perimeter of our island, leaving only a small land force behind. These festivities last for about five days. My informant says the fleet plan to depart for Thormanta in two days."

John Phillip turned to Jim and said, "Skipper, this may be the resister's one chance to strike while the fire's hot. The entire fleet of Viking longships will be gathered in the enemy home port. I figure the invaders will drink and party, just like a bunch of college kids on spring break. With Fredrick's map, we could sneak in to Thormanta after dark in your boat, torch the ships, and beat feet back here before they realize what hit them. Afterward, the resisters could organize a surprise attack on the handful of invaders left behind here in town. A double-whammy, cutting off the enemy supply route and taking back the Utopian seaport. What do you think?"

Jim nodded. "Sounds doable, John Phillip, but let's talk to Fredrick when he returns. We'll need to know the layout of the Thormantan seaport before we move forward."

Both Ben and JT were excited about the idea. The rescuer's enthusiasm was music to Jim's ears, but he also realized everything might change when the harsh reality of the risks involved struck home.

Chapter 25

The *Tristan* rolled like a round-bottom bathtub in the mountainous seas, pounding the wooden ship without mercy. Their sail, torn to shreds by the shrieking gale, streamed downwind like a tattered battle flag. As heavy rain and sea spray pelted the boat, Fredrick crawled on his hands and knees aft to the tiller. He needed to steer the ship, or they would all be tossed overboard into a watery grave.

His mind conjured up the image of the ship's captain, Ericson, as he slipped and fell into the angry, frothing ocean. A heavy roll doomed the senior Viking commander to the deep. The screams of the drowning man were soon lost in the thunderous noise of the howling winds. Now, their longship lay with the side of her hull exposed to the full fury of the sea, the worst position for a vessel in a storm.

Fredrick grabbed the massive tiller with both hands, shouting to the men on the port side. "Men to port, row with all your strength! Pull! Heave! Harder!" The longship turned meter by meter to starboard with stubborn reluctance. He called out again to encourage the oarsmen, straining their arms and backs to turn the dragon-head bow of the ship into the wind and waves.

How much longer could they last? At that moment, he thought of Catherine, remembering her advice to pray to the mysterious God she worshiped if he ran into trouble. So he did. "God, if you can hear me, I beg of you to save this tiny ship and her crew. We do not want to die. Help us." A line of lightning bolts flashed on the horizon, followed by a deafening clap of thunder.

In those brief seconds of illumination, Fredrick sighted the outline of Utopia to the northwest. They were much closer than he thought. Within the hour, the stiff wind dropped to a fresh breeze.

The island helped to block the steep-sided seas, making rowing easier.

Near dawn, the storm passed. The *Tristan* drifted lazily to a stop, rolling gently in the left-over swell. The rowers needed to rest and restore their energy.

Fredrick said, "Ship your oars, men. We are close now, but you need to rest. The land will give us a lee, so we will wait here until sunrise to take her the rest of the way into the Utopian port."

He lashed the heavy steering oar amidships and sat on the thwart seat. So, this was what Catherine meant by faith? To trust in this God, whom she admired so much. He answered Fredrick's prayer with a miracle beyond explanation. In all his years at sea, the young sailor had never seen the wind and waves calm down so fast.

Fredrick leaned against the side of the boat, exhausted. He shut his eyes and was soon sound asleep. A short time later, a powerful hand shook him awake. Opening his eyes, he stared into the sunburned face of a brown-haired, bearded warrior. "Wake up, steersman! On your feet. Take us into the harbor."

The rising sun cast yellows and oranges onto the placid ocean, now flat as a pond, the gentle breeze as soft as the breath of a newborn child. Fredrick stood up, his muscles protesting, his back aching. He removed the rope lashings from the steering tiller, ordering his men to man their oars. The *Tristan* sped along the southern coast of Utopia. His thoughts turned to Catherine, bringing peace to his heart. Soon, he would embrace her in his arms once again.

He touched the back of his boot, feeling the hard dowel with his coded message, still secure, hoping that it too, had survived the driving rain of the great ocean storm.

The tiny vessel made its way to the harbor and slid alongside the wharf. A throng of warriors clapped and cheered wildly as they arrived. The headmaster of the port, a giant of a man named Rolf, with intense blue eyes and a flaming red beard, listened as the crew related the story of how Fredrick saved them from certain death.

He turned to the blond sailor and smiled. "Well done, young Fredrick, well done indeed. You have proven your worth as a leader. And, it just so happens we need a captain for one of our newest ships, the *Valhalla*. You will be her new commander. Be back tomorrow at first light to prepare your ship for sea. We set sail for Thormanta in two days' time."

Forcing himself to appear delighted, Fredrick thanked the man, then walked down the pier to gaze with hatred at the longship he would now command. He wanted nothing more to do with these invaders who had brought death and destruction to this land of peaceful people. From this moment on, he would help Timo and his brave band of resisters in any way possible.

Chapter 26

The five rescuers met in Timo's cottage after hearing Fredrick's story of his perilous journey from Thormanta. They admired the young blond sailor for the risks he took to create a secret code of compass courses and times on each course. This was the key to unlock the door to the home of the enemy.

Fredrick confirmed the invaders were planning a celebration which would last five days. He and the fleet would set sail the day after tomorrow. He expected no invader ships to return to Utopia until after the holiday.

After listening to Fredrick, Timo allowed Catherine to remain at her cottage without a guard. Fredrick would visit with her until dawn the next morning, then depart to prepare his new ship for sea.

Timo stood up from the fire, handing bowls to his guests. "Stew's about ready, so please help yourself to the broth and vegetables from my garden." They filled their plates with the delectable stew and still-warm, sourdough bread. After following Timo in prayers, they dug into the meal with gusto.

John Phillip said, "Jim, I packed a few incendiary devices along with the weapons. These are like a grenade, except they release hot, burning liquid when they explode, causing anything nearby to burst into flames. Now that we know the courses to Thormanta, we can take out their longships with the firebombs while they are drunk from their celebrations. The devices give us additional firepower to make a hit-and-run mission easier."

Are you sure they're ready to face a fire-fight? Sure, they've had a couple of day's training in rugged conditions, but…"

"They'll be ready, Jim. I've worked with lots of men and women in the military, and this group rises to the top in the drills we're putting them through. They're focused, determined, and quick-learners. My suggestion is to take a day off from training tomorrow, select volunteers tomorrow night, then train with just that specific group until the day we depart. I'll let you know if they're fit for a fight before we make a final go, or no-go decision."

After several minutes of discussion, Jim said, "Okay, let's shoot for a departure date of Saturday evening. Fredrick expects the celebrations to begin Thursday night, so two full days of drinking and partying before we arrive should soften up the enemy. We'll go with John Phillip's idea of using fire-bombs to burn the ships at the dock and at anchor. That'll slow them down until they can build new ships, plus the sunken anchored ships will block entry into or out of the harbor. Excellent idea about taking a break, John Phillip. Let's all plan on resting up tomorrow."

The skipper turned to the elder resistance leader and said, "Timo, can you arrange for a meeting in your barn for late tomorrow evening? Let's keep the reason quiet until everyone's together. Sound like a plan?"

Timo puffed on his pipe, pensive for several seconds before he spoke. "Of course, Jim. I will send word for everyone to meet here at 10:00 PM Wednesday night."

Long past sunset, the men ended their discussion and retired for the evening. The adrenaline rush of the upcoming mission filled each of the rescuers with excitement.

Jim endured another sleepless night, tossing and turning, wondering for the hundredth time about the sanity of what was unfolding. And yet, something inside told him he had to take the next step to help the courageous Utopians take back their island.

Chapter 27

JT and John Phillip spent the next day aboard the *Rebecca*, looking over the engine and testing systems. Tilly and Ben hiked to the valley to have a picnic near the waterfall. Jim spent most of the day with Timo, going over the final plans for the mission to Thormanta.

The *Rebecca* could hold fifteen volunteers from the resistance group. All the rescuers would make the trip, including Tilly, who would ride along as ship's medical officer to tend to injuries or illness.

Timo said, "I will pray for the success of your mission, Jim, and for everyone's safe return to Utopia."

"Our greatest advantage will be the hit-and-run tactics, Timo, and, of course, attacking the invaders while many are drunk or off their guard."

Timo nodded, gazing at Jim with sad eyes. "The thought of losing anyone from my group haunts me, thinking back to that time long ago. The massacre in the valley. Now, God has sent you and your brave crew and incredible weapons from the future. So, here we are. My fears fill my heart. If I were not such an old man, I would go with you on your perilous adventure."

Putting his arm around Timo, Jim said, "Old friend, you've contributed more than you realize. You've risked your life day in and day out, offering your resisters a place to meet and talk and hope and dream. To your people, you are a lantern in the darkness."

Tears streamed down Timo's face, his body shaking with emotion, until, spent with fatigue, he said, "I think I'll rest, Jim. Kind of weary. Thank you for your kindness. I'm a silly old man, worried like a mother hen. A few more hours of sleep will do me good."

Jim left Timo alone, walked out into the bright sunshine, and strolled down the road. Two hours later, he hiked into the forest and came upon a crystal-clear brook with smooth, white and tan pebbles lining the bottom. He sat on a fallen tree nearby, staring into the peaceful surroundings. Like Timo, he felt doubt and fear. No challenge in his life topped this one. The crushing weight of the responsibility hit him hard. His crew, Timo and his people—all of their lives—rested in his hands.

Closing his eyes, he prayed. "God, I need your help now more than any time in my life. Hold this brave band of people in your arms. Guide us over the obstacles in our path as we enter the valley of the shadow of death."

The sound of snapping twigs startled him. Grabbing his rifle, he hopped off the log, raising his weapon toward the noise. A beautiful, raven-haired woman with pale, freckled skin stood on the other side of the dense foliage, partially hidden from view. She held a cedar bucket in one hand. Jim watched her kick off her leather sandals, hike up her dress, and wade into the shallow brook. As she turned to make her way back to the bank, their eyes met, and she dropped the bucket, letting out a scream.

Then, just as fast, she recovered from her overreaction. "Oh, hello there! You are Jim, the boat captain from another century. I recognize you from our meeting at Timo's cottage when he introduced your crew to our resistance group. My name's Alexa. Pleased to meet you." Her beautiful smile dimpled the sides of her generous mouth, making her even more lovely.

He picked up the dropped bucket and handed it back to her. "My pleasure to meet you, Alexa. So, do you live nearby?"

She pointed to the north and said, "A short hike from here. I live with my mother in a cottage near the water. You are a long way from Timo's home. So, what brings you here, Jim?"

"No particular reason. I was out for a walk and came across this place, so I stopped to rest."

Alexa smiled again and said, "Yes, it is indeed a beautiful spot. Sometimes I come here to think, to pray, to be alone, or to dream."

Jim nodded and smiled. Alexa sat on the log next to him, placing a hand on his arm. He smelled her scent, sweet earthiness. Her touch electrified and energized him.

"All of us believe God sent you. I do not understand this world you come from, but my heart tells me you and your sailors and the woman Tilly are kind, caring people. Thank you for coming to our world to help us."

Alexa stood, waded into the brook, filled her bucket, and returned to the bank. As she put on her sandals, she said, "Would you like to walk with me to my home, Jim? I would love for you to meet my mother, Patricia. She's fixing a simple meal of cabbage and carrot soup and biscuits. You are welcome to join us if you wish."

"Now, that's the most generous offer I've had all day, Alexa. How could I refuse?" They both laughed as he grabbed her bucket and the two walked hand in hand along the flower-lined path to her mother's cottage.

Chapter 28

"Isn't this lovely, Ben? Not in my wildest dreams could I imagine anything so beautiful." Tilly gazed in wonder at the towering waterfall, the lush green valley, and the wild flowers of red, yellow and blue, bursting in color nearby. She kissed Ben and spread the blanket on the soft carpet of grass. Ben opened the basket and pulled out cheese, bread, and pastries, along with a flask of tropical fruit wine, compliments of Timo.

Tilly said, "I feel like a young girl again, Ben. Timo's tea gives me energy and takes away all my pain. No side effects, and my hair's stopped falling out. Ben, just think what life would be like with no more chemo treatments. Wouldn't that be wonderful?"

Ben stroked her hair, hugging her as he said, "Thank God for that, Tilly. I don't want to lose you, girl."

Tilly broke their embrace, gazed up into his eyes and said, "Darling, I've got a surprise for you. Okay, are you ready? I've got a little one growing inside me."

Ben didn't understand at first as he dug into the meal. "A little what?"

Tilly couldn't help herself. She giggled again and broke into laughter. "No silly, I'm pregnant with your child!"

Ben broke into a massive grin and said, "Holy Toledo, Tilly! You're having a baby? Fantastic, girl! When did you find out?" Ben wrapped his enormous arms around the woman he loved and squeezed her with joy.

"I brought pregnancy kits in my med supplies, tested positive once last night and again this morning. I wanted to make sure before I told you the news. Oh darling, I'm so happy for us. God answered our prayers after all these years of trying. Isn't it wonderful?"

Tears flowed down their cheeks as they laughed and wept together. Ten years of trying and now, in a mystical land called Utopia de Paz, God gave them a miracle. Ben's big hand slid down to his wife's belly, wanting to connect with the tiny heart, with the being inside her, about to grow into a boy or girl. He pushed his wife down onto the blanket, slid the picnic basket over to the side, and held her in his arms.

They soon fell asleep. Not even the thunder of the waterfall could disturb their slumber. In his dreams, Ben played in the park with his children. Tilly sat on the swing with a child in her lap. Another danced with Ben around a gigantic oak tree. Yet another youngster filled the air with her laughter, jumping up and down as children do.

Ben woke up two hours later to find an empty blanket beside him. He looked around but didn't see Tilly. Then he heard the singing, turned toward the stream and saw Tilly bathing. He stripped off his clothes, waded into the water and joined her.

Tilly giggled as he tickled her. They played like two kids, splashing one another, each washing the other's back, and drying off in the late afternoon sun. A gentle breeze wafted through the forest, bringing cool, dry air as the day drew to a close. The two lovebirds finished their meal, packed up, and headed back to Timo's cottage.

They walked hand in hand, talking about the child yet to be born. Making plans for a life yet to be lived, boy or girl, that didn't matter. At that moment, all they cared about was their future as a family, a threesome or foursome, God willing.

But in the back of Ben's mind, a dark shadow of doubt rose like a specter. If they stayed on an island lost in the 19th century, was he risking Tilly and his child to an uncertain future? His mind flashed back to the picture his father gave him to remind him he was never alone. Here, they were surrounded by people who treated each other with dignity and love. In his heart, he realized they'd arrived home, and that's all that mattered.

Chapter 29

Alexa's home overlooked the valley on the edge of the forest. Green wooden shutters trimmed the windows of the white stone cottage. They stepped into a one-room home with a brick-and-mortar fireplace in one corner, and two cots side by side with hand-woven wool blankets on the far wall.

"Jim, this is my mother, Patricia. Mom, meet Jim, the man I told you about. He is the captain of the rescuers who arrived on our island from another world. He and his crew have been teaching our resistance group how to fight the invaders."

Alexa's mother stood and embraced him, then said, "Thank you for being here. I do not understand all Alexa told me. She says you are from another century? Well, no matter, young man. Whoever you are, your eyes tell me you are honest."

Jim thanked the woman, still beautiful in her later years. He guessed her to be in her late sixties or early seventies, with long dark hair, streaked with gray, and snow-white, freckled skin like her daughter's.

Alexa pulled a chair over to the table. "Take a seat, Jim. I've invited Jim for lunch, Mom. I'll serve the food." She walked over to finish the task her mother started. The aroma of the stew and golden-brown, buttery biscuits made his mouth water.

As she prepared their meal, Jim couldn't keep his eyes off Alexa. She moved with the grace of a dancer, all the time talking with him or her mother. He sensed a deep respect between the women.

Patricia patted his hand, jolting him from his gaze. "Jim, you may wonder why a mother would encourage her daughter to join Timo's group of resisters. Long ago, when I was a younger woman, I followed my husband into battle against the invaders. Back then, they showed no mercy toward our people. We fought them for over two years, but in the end, we were overwhelmed. I will never forget the afternoon the messenger arrived with news that my husband and all the remaining fighters had fallen in the Valley of Santa Maria. Now, after years of struggle, you arrive, as if sent by God, to bring hope once again to our island nation. My daughter possesses the strong will of her mother, yet she has a gentle, caring side, too. She will make the right man a fine wife one day." She winked at Jim.

Alexa laughed and said, "Mother, you're embarrassing him! Forgive her, Jim. She tries to play matchmaker. I'm putting that into God's hands, letting him guide me."

Jim figured he'd better steer the conversation in a new direction. He turned to Patricia and said, "Timo told me about the tragedy of the massacre. I'm sorry you lost your husband, Patricia. You and your people have been through so much pain and suffering here. I'm glad we can help you."

After finishing the meal, Jim and Alexa stepped outside into the late afternoon sun; its rays filtered through the trees as it descended toward the western horizon. Alexa grabbed his hand and guided him to the back of the cottage to show off her herb and vegetable garden. Next, they walked hand in hand along the winding path near the bubbling brook.

"So, Alexa, why do you hike so far upstream to fill your bucket when you have fresh water close to your home?"

"The water is so much cleaner farther away. You may have heard the stories about the women who took their own lives, back in the old days. The invaders would kidnap their first-born child, and some mothers could not bear to live without their children. So, they ate the petals of the poisonous needle-and-thorn flower. These white flowers, which look like lilies, grow behind our home. Their petals fall into the water, making it undrinkable. I hike upstream where the flowers are absent, which was where we met earlier today. Perhaps God is telling us something, do you think?" She squeezed his hand as she gazed up at him with her huge, doe-like eyes.

Jim stopped, put his arms around her waist and said, "Alexa, I'm not sure where this is going, but I think we . . ."

She touched him on the cheek and said, "Oh Jim, I understand, and I don't mean to embarrass you. But I'm honest and open and believe in saying what's on my mind. I like you, and you and my mother get along wonderfully." She kissed him lightly on the lips. "Thank you for spending the day with me and my mother. I know this meant the world to her."

Jim hugged Alexa, holding her, feeling the beat of her heart and her strong, lithe body. "Take care, Alexa. I look forward to seeing you and your mother again."

As he walked back to Timo's cottage, Jim felt at peace for the first time in what seemed like forever. This beautiful, compassionate woman filled his heart with a warm glow, making him more determined than ever to help the people of Utopia.

Chapter 30

A gigantic harvest moon greeted the band of revolutionaries as they arrived for the late-night meeting. Timo explained he needed fifteen volunteers for the mission to Thormanta. Twenty-six hands shot high into the air. John Phillip passed out slips of paper, and each volunteer printed their name. JT gathered the papers in a bucket and stirred them with his hand.

Timo drew fifteen names and announced who would take part in the mission. Shouts of joy, along with excited chatter, echoed off the walls of the barn. After several seconds, Timo raised his arms to quiet his people and said, "Remember, there are no obligations. But, if you change your mind, tell me by noon tomorrow, so we can find a replacement. As soon as we know the time of departure, I will send word to the chosen volunteers. Everyone must keep our plans a complete secret. If the invaders discover our intentions, we are doomed. Pray for our success, and may God bless each of you." Timo dismissed his resisters.

John Phillip waited until the last of the group departed. Then, beneath a lantern's light, he unrolled a cream-colored tube of parchment on top of a bale of hay. It showed a detailed sketch of the Thormantan seaport, drawn by Fredrick. The rescuers huddled together to go over the attack plans.

"Four ships are tied up at the wharf, and four are at anchor near the middle of the harbor. The first group will use small rowboats to access the anchored longships, and clamp flammable devices on timers to the hulls. A second group rigs incendiary bombs to take out the four moored ships. The third group plants explosives in the storage sheds near the docks." He pointed to a row of buildings across the street from the moored longships. "Those warehouses should be empty because of the celebration going on in the banquet hall. When everything's in place, all three groups rendezvous on the east end of the port. Fredrick will meet up with us, and we head back to Jim's boat. The explosions will begin a few minutes later. We hop aboard the *Rebecca*, cast off the lines, and steam back to Utopia. If things go as planned, those invaders won't know what hit them. They'll be putting out fires ashore and afloat, plus many of them will be drunk. Skipper, anything you want to add?"

Jim nodded and said, "Tilly and Big Ben will stay on the *Rebecca*, anchored in a secluded cove on the eastern side of the island. Tilly will set up the lower cabin as a surgery center in case we return with wounded. Ben will man the helm, ready to get the boat underway the moment everyone's aboard."

The skipper wrapped up the meeting with the final schedule. "Fredrick says the ships leave Utopia for Thormanta at dawn on Thursday. According to his hourglass recordings, it takes about nine hours to sail to Thormanta, so they should arrive near dusk. The celebrations begin Thursday evening. I'd like to depart at sunset Saturday night. We should make landfall on Thormanta around midnight. Things could change, but that's the plan for now."

The exhausted rescuers crawled under their blankets and were soon asleep. In his dreams, Jim envisioned an auburn-haired girl in the distance lighting a candle and holding it high above her head. She beckoned to him with her hand, as if saying, "Follow the light, Jim, back to my heart." Her beautiful face filled his darkness with a radiant love, sparkling like the rays of the rising sun.

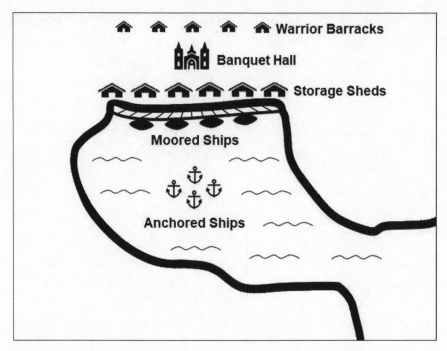

Thormantan Seaport — Fredrick's sketch. Four ships are moored at the wharf and four are anchored. Six storage sheds line the waterfront. The banquet hall (great hall of the chieftains) lies in the center. Warriors preparing for sea or battle live in the barracks.

Chapter 31

The longship *Valhalla* sliced through the waves like a razor-sharp dagger, speeding toward Thormanta with a fresh breeze astern. Fredrick gripped the tiller with both hands, the planned assault by Timo's resistance group weighing heavily on his mind. The warriors under his charge talked of the five days of celebration, with feasts of food and drink, unaware their world would soon turn upside-down in fire.

The young blond sailor dreamed of a time in the not-so-distant future when he and Catherine would marry and have children. No more warrior duties for him. He wanted his own farm, to work the fertile soil with his sons. They would make nets to fish in the crystal-clear streams. And he would learn more about this wondrous God his love worshiped with all her heart.

"Land to port, Captain," shouted the lookout from the bow. Fredrick sighted the faint dark silhouette rising from the sea. He ordered the men to trim the sail for the new steering course, then pushed the heavy tiller to point the ship toward Thormanta.

Near sunset that Thursday evening, the *Valhalla* sailed into the harbor and Fredrick's crew tied her to the wood-planked wharf. He heard the workers on the docks talking with excitement about the holiday celebrations soon to begin.

Stephan, senior captain of the port, met Fredrick on the wharf and asked, "So, did you have a pleasant trip, young Fredrick?"

"Yes, smooth seas and fair winds on the journey. The *Valhalla* is an exceptional vessel. She needs a bit more ballast on the starboard side to correct for a slight list."

"We'll trim your vessel tomorrow, Captain. Finish offloading your supplies; then join us in the banquet hall. Today, we celebrate the founding of Thormanta. Lots of food and drink aplenty! I intend to indulge in both. But the holiday may be shortened, for our leaders received word of an uprising brewing on Utopia. Keep quiet about this for now. Allow your weary crew to relax and enjoy the festivities. We depart in full force in two days to crush this opposition, just like our forefathers did long ago in the Valley of Santa Maria."

Fredrick strained not to show his shock at the dreadful news. His heart filled with fear for Catherine, for Timo and the resisters, and for Jim and the rescuers. He must figure out a way to sabotage the four longships moored next to the wharf. Afterward, he would steal a small sailboat, sail back to Utopia, and warn his friends of the impending invasion.

Raucous laughter and the high-pitched volume of drunken banter boosted the noise level inside the massive banquet room, making Fredrick's ears ring. Thoughts of Catherine helped calm his frayed nerves, drowning out the madness which surrounded him. As the hours wore on, two warriors sitting across from him fell face-first onto their plates, passing out from too much alcohol. He pretended to eat and drink as much as the others, but tossed his meal and beverage onto the dirt floor beneath the table.

Near midnight, Fredrick slipped out of the crowded hall into the cool night air. Halfway down the wharf, he passed a slumbering guard, his back against a wooden barrel, snoring loudly. Fredrick hurried to the end of the pier and stepped aboard the *Valhalla*, making his way to the stern. Using a battle ax, he hacked at the housing, also called a *wart*, which held the steering oar (rudder), on the starboard side of the hull.

In quick succession, Fredrick boarded the three other longships, chopping off the wooden warts with the razor-sharp blade. When finished, he tossed the ax into the sea. As he stepped ashore, another sentry staggered in a drunken zigzag pattern down the wharf.

The intoxicated guard walked up to the dozing sentinel and kicked him in the foot. "Wake up, you fool. If they catch you dozing, they'll whip you. Eric, get up!" The sleeping guard shook his head, rose to his feet, and lumbered back to the great hall for more food and drink.

The half-drunk guard, now on duty, greeted Fredrick with a slight slur in his voice. "Good evening Captain, what are you doing on the docks at this hour? You should take the night off to celebrate with the others."

"Enjoying the night air. I'll return to the hall soon to fill up on more food and drink. What a fine night to honor our gods."

"Yes, it is, Captain. Did you hear the latest rumors? They say a band of revolutionaries on Utopia may try to take back their island." The sentry spat onto the ground, threw his head back, and laughed. "What are they going to fight with? Pitchforks and shovels? My warrior friends tell me we set sail in two days. The chieftains talk of slaughtering every man, woman and child this time. No exceptions! We will paint their island red with blood from one end to the other!"

Chapter 32

Fredrick stood in the shadow of the rope shed, his heart pounding as he waited for the chance to steal one of the smaller sailboats in the harbor. His eyes locked onto the lone sentry, watching the older man's head bob up and down in a drunken stupor as he fought to stay awake.

Finally, the guard dropped his spear onto the ground, slumped against a nearby barrel and dozed off, his soft snores the only sound on this peaceful night. Fredrick stepped out into the moonlight, making his way down the wharf, passing other revelers, sleeping off the drink of the celebration, lying in doorways or on benches.

Near the end of the pier, a thirty-foot sailboat bobbed gently up and down in her slip. After loading the boat with a clay water jug and an hourglass, Fredrick slipped her lines and rowed out into the middle of the harbor.

He raised the square sail in the soft breeze, trimmed the sheets, and sailed swiftly through the port entrance and out into the Gulf. One turn of the glass started the timer for the first leg of his journey. With fair winds, he should sight the island by early afternoon on Friday.

Fredrick steered his first course, aiming the bow on a distant star, watching the hourglass to gauge the time to the next turn. Two hours later, he changed course to the northeast and entered the treacherous, shark-infested waters of the Ferdinand Passage.

His little ship sped along, the fair wind pushing her like a leaf as she skipped over the waves with ease. A short time later, Fredrick turned the boat onto the third leg, pointing the bow due north, aiming at Polaris, the north star. Breakers still pounded the reefs on each side, but they were further away now, posing less of a threat.

Three more hours passed before Fredrick sailed into clear, deep water, leaving the deadly sharks and shoals of the Pass far behind.

He was making much better speed than he first estimated, so he expected to arrive at Timo's lagoon by late morning.

He rounded the bow of his tiny ship up into the wind, doused her sail, and drifted, sipping water from the clay jug at his feet. Although exhausted from sailing his boat alone, he must not allow himself to fall asleep. After rubbing water onto his face, Fredrick hoisted the sail again, pointed his vessel to the north, and continued on his way.

As the sailboat scooted over the gentle waves, thoughts of Catherine flooded his mind. She and every man, woman, and child on Utopia now faced imminent death. How had the invaders found out about the band of resisters? Who was the traitor? So many questions and so few answers. He would let Timo and Captain Jim sort it out.

Fredrick strained his eyes, looking for land, but all he saw was thick haze on the horizon and the emptiness of an endless ocean. Was he lost? Had the strong wind and boisterous waves driven him off course? The sun peeked above the eastern horizon, but no island appeared ahead of the boat.

He shut his eyes, wondering what to do next. High-pitched chirping shook him from his dark thoughts, and he glanced up, seeing a flock of land sparrows streaming across the sky, heading northwest. Fredrick squinted to follow the tiny land creatures to their destination.

And there it was, the faint outline of Utopia de Paz, shimmering through the mist like a beacon, welcoming the weary sailor home from the sea.

Chapter 33

Ben and JT stood on the deck of the *Rebecca*, leaning onto the rail, their coffee mugs filled to the brim. "You guys are having a little one? Wowski, how cool is that?"

Ben grinned and said, "Indeed it is, brother. God blessed us with a child. Can you believe it? Tilly and I couldn't be happier."

The smile dropped from Ben's face the moment he spotted the top of a mast, towering above the palm fronds. Ben tapped JT on the shoulder, pointed and said, "We've got company coming down the channel, shipmate, and they don't appear to be the friendly type."

The young engineer's mouth dropped open as he sighted the wooden mast-pole of an approaching vessel. "Holy freaking Toledo, Ben. Bad guys inbound. Quick! Get the weapons!"

JT and Ben dashed below to grab rifles and ammunition, slid over the side, and waded ashore, taking cover behind a huge, overturned coconut palm tree. As they watched, a red and white square-shaped sail appeared, followed by a sleek wooden hull, gleaming in the sunlight.

Ben whispered, "That's no longship; way too small. Looks about thirty feet at the most."

JT nodded and said, "Wonder if they sent a scout to sniff us out before they attack with the rest of the troops."

They trained their rifles at the figure in the cockpit, fingers ready on the trigger.

"Holy Toledo, Ben, Fredrick's come back!"

Ben's eyes widened as he replied, "Sure enough. What's he doing here?"

JT set his rifle down, picked up the binoculars, and scanned to the left and right.

"You see anyone else aboard?"

"No one else, big guy. Fredrick's alone, and he's not armed. Well, this flushes our mission plans down the toilet. Skipper's not gonna be happy."

Fredrick eased the square sail to allow it to flap in the gentle breeze and the sailboat drifted to a lazy stop alongside the *Rebecca*. He tied the docking lines, lowered the sail, lashed it to the wooden boom, and jumped into the water.

The rescuers met Fredrick at the small beach as he emerged from the water, and all greeted one another with warm hugs.

"Hello, my good friends. I have returned with terrible news of a coming invasion. The Thormantan battle fleet sails for Utopia tomorrow. I must speak to Timo right away."

Ben and JT stared at one another, speechless, knowing this changed everything. As they hurried up the path to Timo's cottage, Fredrick continued. "When I arrived in Thormanta, the shipmaster told me the leaders received word about an uprising on Utopia. They will end the holiday festivities early. The war fleet plans to depart Saturday at noon. Until then, they are celebrating in the banquet hall. Many warriors are already drunk, but that will not stop the invasion force from setting sail. There is talk of total annihilation, and to spare no man, woman, or child."

The three men entered the cottage, finding Timo, Jim, John Phillip and Tilly sitting down to breakfast. All were shocked to see the young blond sailor so soon after his departure.

Fredrick retold his story, adding details on how he disabled the steering oars on the four longships tied up to the wharf. He ended his tale with the theft of the tiny sailing vessel, his passage through the coral reefs, and following the sparrows to Utopia.

Timo tamped a new plug of tobacco into his pipe. "You've risked your life again to help us, Fredrick. This is disturbing news."

Jim added, "Sounds like they're not going anywhere in a hurry, Fredrick. Do I have this right? They can't sail their longships in the state they're in?"

"Yes, the moored ships have no way to steer, turn, or maneuver, so they are unfit for a journey at sea. It will take several days to repair the damaged steering gear, but I didn't have enough time to disable the four vessels at anchor in the cove. I believe they will move the anchored ships to the pier to load warriors and supplies for the invasion."

Jim thought for several seconds. "So, let's say by some miracle, they repair those four ships you damaged within the next two days. Now they have eight ships for a battle fleet. How many invaders might sail for Utopia?"

Fredrick replied, "Each longship can carry thirty men, so perhaps 240 warriors, including battle gear and provisions."

John Phillip turned to the skipper. "Jim, we need to leave for Thormanta as soon as possible. Take advantage of the enemy's sluggishness, and, with all those longships tied up in one place, that'll make burning or blowing them up a lot easier. What do you say?"

"I agree, John Phillip. And Timo, someone in your group collaborated with the enemy. Your resisters are in danger of being arrested if they remain in their homes. Is there a safe shelter where your people can stay while we're away on the mission?"

Timo puffed vigorously on his pipe. "Yes, I know of one secret place on the island, large enough to provide a refuge for everyone. I will speak with my senior resistance members about being on the lookout for suspicious activity. We must locate and stop this spy who is aiding our enemy before they can do more harm."

Chapter 34

Jim turned to the rescuers and said, "Let's plan to leave at sunset tonight. With fair weather, we should arrive in Thormanta near midnight." He unrolled Fredrick's sketch of the Thormantan seaport onto the table. "John Phillip, any suggestions on revisions to your original attack plan?"

The ex-Navy Seal bent down, studying the intricate drawing for several minutes. "So, Fredrick, what is the dominant wind direction we might expect when we arrive at the seaport?"

"Most nights, a steady easterly breeze blows almost parallel to the wharf."

"Okay, good. In that case, Jim, I see only a few minor changes. All eight ships will be tied up in a row along the dock. We stay together, but split up into three teams. Each group enters one of the three warehouses on the west end, setting firebombs on timers. Next, we make our way to the four ships on the east end, and wait for the warehouses to blow up. As soon as that happens, the invaders will be diverted, putting out fires in the sheds. At that point, we hop aboard the longships, rig explosives on ten-minute timers, then head back to the *Rebecca*. Minutes later, those ships burst into flames. The easterly winds should fan the fire down the pier to finish off the four remaining vessels moored to the west. What do you think?"

Jim nodded. "Solid plan, John Phillip. So, Fredrick, are you sure the anchorage cove on the eastern side of Thormanta will still be secure, or should we look for another spot?"

"Yes, Jim, the lagoon is hidden by high sand dunes, so your boat should be safe. The closest guard tower lies two miles farther to the north." He made an X on the map to mark the sentry position.

Timo puffed on his pipe, then turned to the blond sailor and said, "Fredrick, you've done well and your information will save many lives. Catherine is eager to see you again. Return here at dusk to help load supplies and prepare to depart on the mission."

Fredrick thanked Timo and the rescuers, then walked down the dirt path to Catherine's cottage. As he stepped inside the open door, he saw her bent over the fire, pumping the flame with bellows. She turned around as he entered, her hand covering her mouth in shock. "Darling, you're back! What happened?" She threw her arms around him, showering him with kisses.

"I returned to warn Timo and his people. The warrior chieftains found out about his resisters, and they plan to invade Utopia. I escaped last night and sailed back here. I've just come from Timo's cottage. He allowed me to visit you until we depart this evening after sunset."

Catherine gasped. "Oh my God! How do they know about our group?" She touched his face with concern in her eyes. "Who would betray us?"

Timo had insisted that she stay inside her home with Tilly the entire time Fredrick was away. This new turn of events might convince the senior resistance leader to trust her enough to rejoin the fight with her neighbors to win their freedom and start a new life with the man she loved.

Leading him over to the table, she said, "You are safe, my love, which gives me peace. Please, sit down; you look so weary. I will make you breakfast. Tell me about your perilous journey."

He began with the trip back to Thormanta on the *Valhalla*, and how the captain of the port and the drunken guard revealed the plans of the impending invasion. As they ate, he described how he disabled the ships moored in the harbor, and escaped in a small sailboat to return to Utopia.

"We leave tonight after sunset, Catherine. Jim says we must go now to destroy the ships before they can set sail for Utopia. Timo will move you and the rest of his people to a secure haven while we are gone. You cannot stay here, my love. I trust Timo to keep you safe while I am away."

She nodded, not knowing what else to say, realizing whatever she said would not make any difference. In a few hours, the man she loved with all her heart would depart once again, gone on a mission which could change the course of Utopian history. They finished their meal in silence, comfortable in each other's presence.

Fredrick stretched out on the small cot in the corner, shut his eyes, and was soon fast asleep. Catherine sat on one end, her hands stroking his blond locks, her tears falling on the soft pillow. How many more times could the love of her life enter the valley of the shadow of death and return unscathed? She must trust in God now more than ever to shield him from the fiery wrath of the dragon warriors.

Chapter 35

Alexa and Jim walked along the banks of the brook to the fallen tree where they first met. As soon as they sat down, he told her the story of Fredrick's harrowing journey. The moment he finished, she gasped and said, "If we have a traitor in our group, this puts everyone in mortal danger. How soon before the invaders come looking for us?"

"We are taking no chances. Timo knows of a safe place a few miles from his cottage. Everyone who stays behind will take shelter there until we return from our mission. There will be plenty of food, weapons, and supplies to last several weeks."

"No, Jim, we will stay here. My mother is much too old to travel. She and I will remain at our home."

Jim shook his head. "Alexa, you and your mother must leave. No one is safe staying in a cottage. Timo has a mule and wagon to carry supplies and family members to the hideout. Each of you must pack one bag right now. Do you want me to explain the situation to your mother or would you rather tell her yourself?"

Alexa fell silent for several moments. "Alright, Jim, I trust your advice and will do as you say. I will talk to my mother, but please walk with me back to my home." Holding hands, they strolled in silence until they arrived at the front door of her cottage.

He held her close one more time, feeling the beat of her heart, wanting to stay, but realizing she had to handle this in her own way. "Take care of yourself, Alexa. Timo will send the cart for you and your mother later this afternoon."

She gazed up at him, her eyes glistening with tears as she said, "I will pray for you, Jim, and for everyone sailing with you tonight. Come back to me." She kissed him lightly on the forehead, turned, and disappeared into the tiny home. Jim stood at the doorway for a few seconds, electrified by this strong, compassionate woman who tugged at his heart, filling him with warmth every time he was around her.

He jogged back to Timo's cottage to help load the wagon with supplies to transport to the new shelter, a cave near the waterfall. Two hours later, the cart was filled to overflowing.

After hitching Galapagos to the bridle, they climbed up onto a wooden plank which served as a seat. Timo took the reins, and within an hour, they arrived at the bottom of the waterfall. He winked at Jim, then pointed to the top of the falls. "The entrance lies on the other side of that curtain of water. Quite difficult to spot from our present location, don't you think?"

Squinting to see through the thick, white sheet of descending water, Jim shook his head. Timo clapped him on the shoulder, grinned and said, "Hidden like a chameleon, my fine friend. Come, I will show you."

They tied the mule to a tree trunk, and the elder resistance leader led Jim up a steep path over rocky terrain bordered by colorful flowers. The sound became deafening as they approached the peak. He followed Timo to a narrow footpath less than ten meters wide, running behind the cascading waterfall.

The massive cliff wall opened into a gigantic cavern, illuminated by filtered sunlight streaming through the entryway. The moment they rounded a sharp bend near the entrance, the thunderous noise outside dropped to a mere whisper. Jim stared in wonder at the enormity of the cave, the stony ceiling at least twenty feet overhead, and the cliff walls as far apart as a school cafeteria.

"Amazing, Timo. So quiet a baby could fall asleep in here. Huge and well hidden." He noted torches lining the walls on each side. "Better still, you and your resisters have the advantage of the high ground. Easy to see anyone approaching."

Timo nodded. "Yes, Jim. Only one other person has been to this secret cave. You know her as Alexa's mother, Patricia. She and I came here long ago, a few years after her husband died. We stumbled across it by chance one stormy day." Timo looked pensive for several moments. "Let's get the cart unloaded, and I'll tell you more, which I believe you need to know."

It took the better part of an hour for the two men to transport the provisions, rifles, and ammunition to the cavern. When they finished, the elder resistance leader sat on a bench, lit his pipe, and told Jim the rest of his story.

After the massacre in the Valley of Santa Maria, Timo helped Patricia recover from her grief. They became close friends and took long walks together. For two years, they had walked near the waterfall, but never noticed the cave. One day, he and Patricia came to the falls with blankets and food for a picnic.

Minutes after they arrived, the heavens burst open with a torrential downpour. Grabbing their provisions, they hiked up the path toward the top of the cliff, looking for shelter. They stumbled upon the cavern entirely by the grace of God. The rains continued into the evening, so they stayed for the night, crawling under the blanket, huddling together to keep warm in the chilling cold. Nine months later, Patricia gave birth to a beautiful baby girl, whom they named Alexa.

Chapter 36

Timo and Jim moved everyone into the cave by late afternoon. Twenty people would make the stone fortress their home for the next two days. The elder resistance leader appointed four senior men to maintain order, ration the supplies of food, and schedule round-the-clock guard duty.

They would post sentries at staggered distances along the top of the cliffs to warn of approaching danger. Timo cautioned them that a traitor may be among the group. "Keep the secret of a collaborator to yourselves, men. There is no need to create panic or paranoia, which can lead to finger-pointing or worse. All our lives depend on complete secrecy, so allow no one to leave without my permission."

Timo's hidden refuge was now open knowledge among his people. If anyone left the cavern to return home or revealed the resister's location to the enemy, they all faced capture, torture, or even death.

Jim hugged Timo one last time and made his way back to the cottage. When he arrived, John Phillip and the crew were busy loading rifles, ammunition, and explosive charges onto the *Rebecca*. The last rays of the sun peaked through the foliage near the lagoon. A southerly wind whistled through the palm trees, promising a bumpy passage to Thormanta that night. Tilly passed around medication for seasickness to all aboard. She was taking no chances on seasickness, which could lead to severe dehydration.

"All set, Skipper," said John Phillip as he and the resisters lashed and secured the last of the cargo below in the cabin. "Looks like we're in for a rough ride tonight?"

Jim nodded in agreement. "Yep, winds from the south, so we're heading dead into the waves on the first part of our trip; then we'll take them abeam as we round the coral reefs. But *Rebecca* is a stable boat, and we'll keep our speed slow to give us a smoother ride."

The diesel roared to life with a deep-throated rumble as JT popped up onto the deck from the engine room. "Man, oh man, I love this machine. Sweet to work on and easy to access. I tweaked the idle, so she should purr like a kitten. Ready to rock when you are, Skip." As usual, the young mechanic was grinning like a Cheshire cat, excited to be back in his element.

The skipper gave JT a thumbs-up, then strolled to the bow where Big Ben was preparing the docking lines for casting off. "How's Tilly doing, Ben? Are you sure she's up to this?"

"Tilly's glad to be here, Skip. No pain, no fever, and no sleepless nights since she started drinking Timo's tea. Don't know what that stuff does, but it's a miracle. God's given Tilly a second chance and blessed us with a little one growing inside her. So, yea, she's raring to go."

As he made his way back to the pilothouse, Jim glanced up at the cloud-filled sky, noticing a row of stars popping out through the blackness like tiny dome lights in a theatre. No moon tonight, which meant more cover to hide their approach to the enemy camp in Thormanta.

Jim stepped inside the cabin, stood behind the wheel, gave the signal to cast off, and Ben slipped the mooring lines. The crew at the stern pulled in the anchor. He shifted the engine into reverse and backed the *Rebecca* out of the channel and pivoted her to starboard. The trawler's varnished bow rose like a graceful swan as Jim pushed the throttle up to full speed and steadied onto a southerly course.

Fredrick stood next to the helm, mouth opened in awe. "This is quite a fine ship, Captain," he said with an ear-to-ear grin. "Much easier to maneuver than with oars or sails!"

"Yes, she's a joy to handle, Fredrick. I love to sail, but I do it for fun, not as a profession. Would you like to steer her? I'll take over the navigation. Go ahead, take the wheel."

The blond sailor jumped onto the helm seat and soon had the boat steady on the first course. His face showed contentment, yet sadness. Jim put his hand on Fredrick's shoulder. "Catherine is in excellent hands, Fredrick. God and the resisters will keep her safe and sound."

His own doubts and fears filled his mind, and he swallowed hard, wondering once again about the sanity of what they were doing. His mind drifted to Alexa, remembering the sweetness of her kisses. Jim whispered a silent prayer for guidance, for watching over Timo and his people, and for protecting the rescuers and the volunteers aboard his boat.

Stepping out onto the deck, Jim leaned against the rail, gazing out at the ruffled whitecaps, breathing the salty air deep into his lungs to calm his nerves. Five minutes later, he returned to the cabin to plot the next steering course to take the *Rebecca* and her crew to Thormanta, home of the dragon warriors.

Chapter 37

Timo checked on the guard positions stationed near the cave entrance at the base of the hill. Each sentry would stand duty for two hours. He sat down and prayed for his friends and neighbors and for Jim and his crew. His heart was heavy with the strain of responsibility and doubt, wondering if he was up to the task. Was he too old? Movement nearby woke him from his reverie.

He looked up and smiled as he said, "Well, hello there, Patricia. God must have plans to bring us together like this. Please, come and sit with me. You are looking well, as is Alexa, beautiful as always. The two loveliest women on the island, no doubt." Patricia's glowing skin and bright eyes made her look ten years younger.

She put her hands on his shoulders and kissed the top of his head. "Hello, dear. You were always a tease, with your charming sense of humor. Yes, we are both well. Scared, of course, but otherwise in fine health. Thank you for asking." She sat next to him, taking his hand in both of hers. "I pray we defeat the invaders this time. Just think, Timo, you and I can marry. Wouldn't that be wonderful, dear?" She touched his face gently, kissing him lightly on the cheek.

Timo smiled and nodded. "Yes, indeed. We'll be the first marriage they record on the day it happens."

Thormantan law prohibited Utopian widows from re-marrying. The invaders enforced this decree to reduce the birth rate on the island. Fewer births meant less threat from future generations who might attempt to retake their conquered lands. If the resisters won back their freedom, Timo and Patricia could share a life together, a dream they'd talked about for almost twenty years.

"You have cared for us all this time, Timo. Alexa loves you with all her heart. Her prayers always include our reunion as a family one day. Without you, we would be beggars, living on the street. But you built our cottage and cared for us as if we lived together. All this time, we have kept our secret to ourselves."

"Patricia, I am happy for you and Alexa. She's quite taken with Jim. An outstanding young man, full of vim and vigor. But you realize he comes from a different time and place?"

She squeezed his arm. "Alexa has talked of nothing but Jim for the past two days. It reminds me of my feelings for you. Do you remember? Those eyes of yours! They had a magnetic attraction which a young girl found irresistible. And, oh my, so handsome and strong! You still are, my dear."

"Did you not hear me, Patricia? Jim plans to leave soon. I told you about this black crescent which appears in the Gulf, visible for only thirty days every twenty years. After that, it disappears into the sea for another two decades. I could never prove the theory until Jim and his crew appeared, not once, but twice. You must realize this union between Jim and our daughter cannot last. He must return to his world in the 21st century in a few days."

She shook her head. "I don't know how to tell Alexa. What do I say? How do I tell her that this brave, strong, kind man she loves from another world must go back in a week's time?"

Both lovers sat in silence, holding hands, each lost in their thoughts. Patricia finally spoke, her voice choked with emotion. "I will ask Jim to talk to Alexa when he returns. This will break her heart, but I see no other way."

Patricia stood, kissed and hugged Timo one more time, then turned and made her way back to the cavern. The old man's tears flowed down his face, and his body shook with grief. All this time lost, living apart from the woman he loved. The spark, still there, the flame, still bright.

He also wept for Jim and Alexa, two lonely people who, like Timo and Patricia, met and fell in love when neither time nor place made sense. These two young people would soon have to face the reality and heartbreak of leaving one another behind an impenetrable wall. The pain and heartache of love and loss, like a shadow, here for a flash in time, gone in an instant.

For him and Patricia, time was running out. He imagined the sand in an hourglass, sifting through the slender neck into the chamber below. Its speed increasing day by day. How long did they have before death came rapping on their door?

He shook the black thoughts from his head. There would be time for love and regret later, but for now, he must focus on his responsibilities to his people. Timo walked back to the cave, his head held high. God had chosen him for this mission, and he would not fail.

Chapter 38

Storm clouds hovered near the seaport of Thormanta as the wind whistled through the rigging of the Viking ships, straining at their moorings like restless stallions. Gunnar, the blacksmith, passed on his assessment of the damage fittings to Stephan, senior captain of the port.

"Two more days to repair the destroyed parts, Captain. He crushed the warts which hold the steering oar. The damage is so great to the wood, we must forge new ones from iron. They will support the rudder until you return from your journey, when we can make permanent repairs."

Stephan shouted in rage. "The traitor Fredrick will pay for this, a slow death if I have my way with him. Well, hurry with your task, blacksmith. We sail in two days and I will listen to none of your excuses."

Gunnar held back his anger at being insulted. Returning to his work, he hammered on the pulsating red metal. Sparks flew and sweat from his labor dripped onto the hot coals of the open fire pit.

The port captain moved down the wharf to the next longship in line. Each vessel revealed a similar problem, a smashed steering gear.

Stephan thanked the gods for the Utopian collaborator named Benjamin, who slipped a note to one of the longship captains before they sailed for Thormanta. Upon arrival, he passed the information to Stephan, who immediately briefed the council leaders. The note gave intimate details of the Utopians' planned uprising.

The chieftains came to the same conclusion. They would return to Utopia, round up the resisters, and set an example with public executions. Line the roads with their impaled bodies, lashed to crosses, like the son of that God they worshiped. Strike fear into the rebels, so this would never happen again.

But, before they could arrest Fredrick, he escaped in a stolen harbor transport boat. Stephan seethed, spittle flying as he gazed skyward, shouting, "I pray to you, Aegir, god of the sea, that his boat was dashed onto the coral reefs to the east, a fitting death for a deserter. May the sharks devour his foul body one limb at a time. Turn the sea crimson red with his blood." He stomped off to meet with other captains in the council house to complete plans for the upcoming raid on Utopia de Paz.

At that moment, the subject of Stephan's wrath stood at the helm of the *Rebecca*. As the boat pounded into the eight-foot waves, Fredrick eased the wheel to take the force of the seas to the side. Jim watched the talented sailor steer his cabin cruiser like a pro, and she responded with the grace of a ballerina.

The crew and passengers braced themselves on the handholds below. Tilly came up the ladder, stepped into the pilothouse and said, "A few minor seasick folks, Jim, but most of the guys are hanging in there."

Jim nodded. "Thanks for the update, Tilly. Keep everyone rested and hydrated. We should be through the worst of the weather soon."

Ben appeared next to Tilly, holding on to the overhead handrail. "Got a small leak in the forward bilge, Skip. Nothing to be too concerned about, but going dead into the seas loosens things up. I've tightened the fitting down, so it's just a trickle."

He followed the big man below to check the problem. An inch of water stood in the narrow cavity of the hull. The pump hummed, sucking water into a hose and expelling it overboard. "Seems to be okay, Ben. Let me know if it gets any worse."

As Jim climbed the ladder up to the pilothouse, JT shouted from the bow, "Breakers to port and starboard!" Jim dashed out the door, squinting into the pitch-black starless night, sighting white water boiling on top of the waves, only a quarter mile ahead.

He stepped back into the cabin, studying the chart as he said, "Fredrick, are you certain this is the correct course to take us through the shoals?"

The young sailor nodded. "Yes, here we enter the Ferdinand Passage. It resembles a narrow neck which lies between the coral heads. I have navigated this channel many times and will keep your vessel and her crew safe."

"Good enough, Fredrick. You're my pilot. So, you estimate two more hours before we exit the passage?"

"Yes, Jim, after we clear the shoals, we turn west to take us to Thormanta. We make excellent time in your fast ship, and she steers like a dream!" It surprised Jim that Fredrick showed no fatigue, but since he wanted to continue steering, he left him at the wheel.

As the *Rebecca* entered the pass, Jim concentrated on the depth sounder, his eyes glued to the yellow digital numbers, which never fell below sixty feet. Two hours later, they shot through the other side into deeper, calmer water. Fredrick turned the boat to the west. Jim expected more rolling than before, but the reefs to the south created a natural lee, helping to calm the boisterous seas and give everyone a much-needed break.

Five minutes later, JT shouted from the bow. "Land dead ahead, Skip!" Grabbing his binoculars, Jim stepped outside, bracing his elbows on the cabin top. The dark outline of Thormanta rose from the ocean beneath the overcast sky. He signaled Fredrick to slow down as they approached the land of the enemy.

Chapter 39

Catherine and Alexa spent most of the day together, talking of newfound love, sharing their fears for the men who had touched their hearts. Now near midnight, the two women huddled under their blankets in one corner of the cave, speaking in whispers. The flicker of torches at the far end of the tunnel showed they were not the only ones unable to sleep.

"When did you find out Timo was your father, Alexa?"

"My mother told me when I turned ten. Before, I always wondered why she and Timo were such close friends, but they never married. All these years, we lived apart because of these cruel laws enforced by our oppressors."

Catherine replied, "If Jim and the resisters destroy the enemy in their home, the law will change. Your mother and father will reunite and marry. You must keep telling yourself these things will come to pass. I find faith and hope keeps me going, Alexa. Otherwise, life becomes unbearable."

Catherine paused as tears clouded her eyes. "I lie awake at night, worrying about Fredrick. So strong and virile, yet, also warm and kind. My mind conjures up terrifying images of what could happen to him if he's captured. By now, the invaders back in Thormanta will know about the ships he disabled. If he's arrested, they will show no mercy."

Alexa hugged her friend and said, "He's not alone this time, Catherine. Jim and his crew and the brave group of resisters are with him. I'm not sure about God's intentions, but my mother reminds me to be patient. She says God works on his schedule, not ours. We have these amazing weapons from the 21st century and the training to use them. Before he left, Jim said we alone must now choose freedom or serfdom."

She glanced over at her sleeping mother and smiled. "I did not understand what he meant until my mother explained. This brave band of rescuers from another world risked everything to come here, bringing supplies, rifles, and training. They have shown us the door to our freedom. We have three choices. If we leave the door closed, we continue to live in fear. If we open the door to peek inside but take no action, our lives will remain the same. But, if we step over the threshold to the other side, we gain the power to change our future."

The women embraced one another in silence, absorbing the words of Alexa's mother, a woman of immense beauty, kindness, and wisdom, sleeping just a few feet away.

Catherine nodded. "Thank you for sharing this story, Alexa. You have opened my mind to what drives Fredrick to do what he does. Perhaps I will sleep better knowing no matter what happens today, we have taken the third option. We are on the right path."

Soon, both women drifted asleep next to one another. Catherine dreamed of sunlight, puffy cotton-ball clouds and a cozy cottage in a valley near a bubbling brook. Her son with curly blond hair ran after his giggling sister until they fell on the ground, their shouts of joy musical in its sweetness.

Fredrick picked up his children, turning them round and round in circles. They squealed with delight; then they were off, chasing one another in a game of tag.

He came over to her, wrapped his muscular arms around her slender waist, and kissed her deeply on her lips. She broke away, pushed him playfully, daring him to catch her. They chased one another down to the brook where the children were playing.

Out of the corner of her eye, she noticed hundreds of tiny dots appear on the hills surrounding their valley paradise. The dots grew larger as a swarm of angry warriors, dressed in full battle gear, charged toward them. She screamed in terror as arrows rained down on her family, piercing flesh, destroying everything she loved, cherished, and adored before her eyes.

Chapter 40

As the *Rebecca* approached Thormanta, rain fell in sheets, pounding the glass windshield of the pilothouse, lowering visibility to less than half a mile. Jim concentrated on the radar, which showed a crystal-clear picture of the eastern side of the island.

"Ben, take the wheel. Fredrick, you can help me navigate the boat to the cove where we will anchor."

The blond sailor hovered next to Jim, looking over his shoulder, mesmerized by the image on the scope, which appeared as a fine, detailed yellowish-green outline on a black background. "Your magic radar instrument sketches a much better map than mine, Jim. If we were in a longship in this gale, we would turn into the wind to stop until the storm passed. Otherwise, we might wreck upon the reefs." He pointed to a spot two miles away. "The elders tell stories of shipwrecks, their crews eaten by the great gray sharks which live in the Ferdinand Passage."

Fredrick paused as he watched the sweep of the radar antenna on the scope. "So, Captain, what is our distance to Thormanta?"

Jim checked the range. "About three miles off right now."

Shaking his head, Fredrick said, "You must get closer, Captain. Turn northwest until you are one mile away, then steer to the northeast to sail parallel to the island until we can locate the inlet."

Jim directed Ben to steer the *Rebecca* onto the new compass course, watching the scope and depth sounder. When within a mile of the beach, they turned to hug the rugged coastline. The water-depth plummeted from over 200 feet to 36 feet.

Fredrick concentrated on the radar picture. "Ah yes, much better. I would sail this direction until the cove appears. We are fortunate to have the cover of rain and darkness. Sentry towers are staggered about five miles apart along the perimeter of the dunes. However, at night the guards become lax and doze at their posts."

Jim had forgotten about the watchtowers from the earlier briefing. On a clear night with a bright, full moon, his boat would stand out like a white dot on a blackboard. But not tonight. The black sky and driving rain would hide them like a shroud.

A short time later, a sliver of land appeared as a tiny crevice in the otherwise solid profile of the island. Fredrick confirmed this to be the opening leading to the anchorage.

Jim relieved Ben on the wheel, sending him forward to help JT prepare the anchor. John Phillip and the resisters manned each side of the vessel with rifles at the ready, scanning for threats as they crept into the canal at a snail's pace. By the time they entered the lagoon, the squall had moved out to sea, and only a light drizzle remained.

The depth sounder dropped to twelve feet of water beneath the keel. Jim stopped the *Rebecca* and shouted through the open pilothouse window. "Okay guys, let her go!" Ben and JT released the brake from the windlass. The chain ran out and the heavy anchor splashed into the water.

As the skipper reversed the engine, the plow-shaped anchor dug deep into the sandy seabed. After stopping the engine, all became as quiet as the inside of a cathedral, a gentle breeze ruffling the tattered flag astern.

The crew lowered the ten-foot dinghy alongside, loaded it with supplies, and Ben transported the assault team and their equipment to shore. He wished them well and returned to join Tilly aboard the *Rebecca*.

Jim asked John Phillip to brief everyone again on the mission plan. The resisters gathered around as the ex-Navy Seal spread the map on the ground, lighted by the red glow of his headband light.

Pointing to the first group of buildings to the west, he said, "We set our incendiary bombs here, here, and here. Three targets on ten-minute timers. Next, we head down the wharf to the vessels moored to the east. We wait for the sheds to explode. As soon as they do, we jump aboard the four longships, rig more explosives on short timers, then hike back to Jim's boat. A few minutes later, the ships burst into fireballs, igniting the wooden pier, which burns like a fuse down to the remaining dragon ships tied up on the west end. Questions?"

All remained quiet, lost in their private thoughts. The skipper led the group in prayer, choosing the 23rd Psalm, remembering that first night at Timo's cottage. Tonight, those words of comfort carried an ominous message, for they would soon enter the valley of death, home of the fire-breathing dragons of his dreams.

Chapter 41

"Wake up, Timo."

A heavy hand shook the elder resistance leader until he rolled onto his back, opened his eyes and said, "Is it my turn for sentry duty?"

His close friend and neighbor Thomas knelt next to him. "I believe Benjamin is the traitor, Timo. He was on guard duty with us this evening, but now he's gone. Vanished!"

Timo sat up, shocked by the news. "What are you saying? How do you know this to be true? Tell me what happened."

"Thirty minutes ago Benjamin asked Davis to cover his position because he needed to relieve himself. He disappeared around a boulder and never returned. Davis and I scouted the area, but found no trace."

Timo stood and said, "Wake up Garth, Hendrick, and Ivan. Tell them to be ready to go in ten minutes with weapons and ammunition. You will remain here, Thomas. Return to your post and tell no one else until we find out more."

After getting dressed in warm clothes and his heaviest coat, Timo grabbed his rifle, walked over to the ammo crates, and loaded rounds into the weapon. Stepping outside, he gazed skyward at the blanket of stars twinkling like tiny fireflies. The light from the heavens would help them track down the missing man.

His thoughts turned to Catherine and Alexa, his friends and neighbors, and Jim and those on the mission in Thormanta. If Benjamin told the invaders about the hidden cave, they were doomed. If that meant death to a collaborator, so be it.

Timo caught himself, wondering how this anger had boiled to the surface after being buried inside all these years. He remembered the heart-rending loss of his friends who perished long ago in the massacre at Santa Maria. He could not allow that to happen ever again.

Strolling back into the cave, he set his rifle down and opened the wooden crate in the corner, pulling out four of the gruesome weapons. John Phillip called these *combat knives*. He said they had one purpose; to kill a man in silence. Timo strapped one of the heavy steel tools of death to his hip. As he walked out into the cool night air, the three men of the pursuit party stood near the entrance, whispering among themselves.

Timo said, "Put these knives on your belts now. If we must take a life, we do so in silence. Your rifles are secondary because the noise of gunfire might reveal our position. Do not use any weapon, knife or firearm, except as a last resort. We must first find out what Benjamin has revealed to the invaders."

After the men finished strapping on their weapons, he continued. "We do not know the route Benjamin took, but he is not familiar with this area, so I must assume he will follow the stream. He has the advantage of a head start, so we will use a shortcut."

Timo led the band of resisters to the bottom of the incline and turned south, using the stars to guide him in the desired direction. He increased the pace to a jog. "Too old for this," he whispered to himself as his breathing became more difficult. Fear drove him onward.

Ivan shouted from the rear. "Timo, over here! A piece of cloth snagged on a thorn bush. I recognize this as Benjamin's winter coat, which he wore tonight on guard duty."

The senior resistance leader studied the crimson-colored wool fabric. "Yes, an excellent sign, but it also tells me he found out about this shortcut. We must hurry." They had one advantage over the collaborator. He walked with a pronounced limp from a childhood illness, so running was out of the question.

Timo prayed for more clues to help them find Benjamin. Could he make it to the invader camp at the Utopian port before they caught him? He set his worry aside, concentrating on the task at hand. Within minutes, he spotted trampled ground and faint footprints, veering to the right off the main path.

"Hurry, this way, men. He will follow the stream which runs along the edge of the forest. We are close, so remember, no gunfire. Once we capture Benjamin, we will question him. Then, and only then, do we decide his fate."

As the four men rounded the tree line, starlight revealed a figure rustling through the dense foliage, limping with each step. The man appeared exhausted, making slow progress. Benjamin heard his pursuers behind him, turned and cried out in fear. He jumped into the icy stream, stumbling and tripping in the knee-deep water as he dashed for the other side.

Timo shouted, "Ivan, stay here in case he turns around. Garth and Hendrick come with me."

The three men sloshed through the shallow water, climbed onto the opposite bank, and trained their weapons on Benjamin. Now realizing they had him boxed in, the suspected traitor stopped midstream, raising both arms high into the air in surrender.

With the speed of a mountain lion, Ivan plunged into the brook, his knife held high, eyes filled with fury. Benjamin screamed in terror as the resister grabbed him by his curly black hair, pulling his head back, the glistening steel blade hovering inches above his throat.

Chapter 42

Timo shouted to Ivan to stop, but the man's madness deafened him to the command. Garth jumped into the stream, reaching the crazed resister seconds before he could draw his blade across the prisoner's throat. He grabbed Ivan, pulling him back hard, and the knife fell from his slippery hands.

The terrified Benjamin raced to the bank nearby, where Timo and Hendrick pulled him out of the water. Exhausted, Benjamin collapsed, gasping for air, shaking with fear.

Ivan screamed in rage. He pummeled Garth with his fists, but he was no match for the bigger man, who slapped Ivan's face again and again to calm him.

Garth shouted, "Stop, fool. Enough!"

Ivan's anger subsided, and he pushed Garth's hand away, waded back to the shore, and sat on the bank.

After ordering Hendrick to move Benjamin out of the way and stand guard duty, Timo walked over to Ivan and said, "You disobeyed my orders. One more incident like that and you become our second prisoner. I will not tolerate disobedience on a mission. Too many lives are at stake. Set aside your personal feelings. Justice will prevail, but not like this. We must find out what he has communicated to our enemy. Do you understand?"

Ivan nodded. "I lost my head. This will not happen again. I was thinking of Tamara and Celia and what this traitor may have done to their safety." Ivan's wife died in childbirth. He had raised his two daughters, now ten and twelve, by himself.

Timo motioned for the other two resisters to join them. "I will question our prisoner alone. Garth, Ivan, and Hendrick—spread out along the bank of the stream to watch for danger."

After they were out of hearing range, the elder resistance leader knelt and spoke in a soft voice. "Benjamin, you have one minute to tell me what you passed on to the invaders. If you do not, I will turn the interrogation over to these men, who will cut you into pieces. They will not hesitate, so tell me everything. If you try to deceive me, I will walk away leaving you to your fate."

With a trembling voice, the captive told his tale of treachery. He had slipped a note to one of the longship captains before they set sail for Thormanta, listing all the names of the resisters. Tonight, he was on his way to warn those left behind of the mission to destroy the longships in their home port. His intentions were to lead them back to the hidden cave.

In return for spying on his people, the Viking chieftains promised Benjamin a new life for his family in Thormanta. He would have a new cottage, a plot of fertile farmland, and never again live under the shadow of hunger or poverty.

Timo shuddered as he thought about what might have happened if they had not caught the collaborator in time. He waved Hendrick over, telling him to stand guard over their prisoner while he spent a few minutes in contemplation.

Hiking a short distance into the forest, Timo sat on a log, closed his eyes and prayed for guidance. Would Jim and the assault team have time to stop the invaders before they returned with a war fleet to unleash their bloody wrath on the Utopian resisters?

Chapter 43

The seaport of Thormanta was quiet except for a handful of workers aboard the disabled ships. The leaders may have shortened the holiday celebrations, but the warriors still drank their grog and gorged themselves on the mounds of food.

Fredrick led the resisters to the three sheds on the west side of the harbor. They split up into three groups to set the incendiary devices. Jim's team entered a storage warehouse, buried one bomb beneath a wagon filled with barrels of fish oil, and another under a cart stacked with coils of rope and wooden blocks.

They checked that all was clear and stepped into the street, staying in the shadows, waiting for the others to finish their part of the mission. A sentry passed near the second building. He appeared to be drunk and staggered from side to side like a lazy hermit crab.

Stopping outside a warehouse, the Viking guard propped his spear to the side, turned and urinated against the wall. When finished, he picked up his weapon, crossed the cobbled road, and continued his rounds.

"Where did he come from, Skipper?" said James, a tall redhead and the youngest member of their team. Jim raised a finger to his lips to urge the inquisitive youngster to keep quiet.

The guard stumbled past the building where John Phillip and his squad were inside, rigging explosives on timers. Jim pushed the light button on his wristwatch. The green glow of the nightlight showed only six minutes remained before their hiding place would explode into flames. All three groups needed to get moving.

A few moments later, the second group left the middle building. By the time the ex-Navy Seal and his team opened the door of the third building and stepped outside, the sentry had turned the corner and was no longer in sight.

The assault team moved together, staying in the shadows, crouching as they approached the four ships moored on the eastern end of the wooden wharf. Fredrick pointed to the last shed on the pier and said, "We will hide in this deserted warehouse until the bombs explode in the three buildings to the west."

Less than two minutes passed before the first bomb detonated, blowing the roof of the building skyward, erupting in splinters of wood and flame. Without delay, the two other structures burst into yellow-orange fireballs. The night came alive as half-dressed warriors poured from the barracks and banquet hall, shouting in panic as they rushed toward the burning buildings.

Peeking out the window, Jim watched as the guard they sighted earlier scampered past, eager to join his comrades to fight the raging fires, now threatening to destroy their fleet. The Vikings passed out buckets, filling them with water from the harbor, but intense heat and choking smoke forced the firefighters to retreat.

Jim scanned for other sentries nearby, but as predicted, the burning structures served as diversions to keep the warriors occupied. The teams hurried across the empty street, and the skipper's group boarded the first and second vessels to rig their firebombs. John Phillip led the other groups onto the two remaining longships, planting detonators at the bow and stern of each vessel.

Everyone gathered at the warehouse across the street. The skipper made one final head count to ensure they were leaving no one behind. "Okay, let's head home. Fredrick, lead the way."

A quarter mile away, the bombs on the first ship ignited, sending a shockwave through the air. They all looked back as the second, third and fourth longships blew apart in succession. The wooden pier caught fire, burning like a giant fuse, fanned by the strong easterly wind to engulf the vessels to the west.

Fingers of reddish-orange flame soared skyward, casting yellowish light on the rooftops of the Thormantan village. The resisters hurried toward the *Rebecca,* increasing their pace to a jog. As they climbed the tall dunes surrounding the cove, two men at the rear shouted, "Skipper, invaders coming this way!"

Jim turned, sighting a dozen warriors closing in fast, less than half a mile behind. "Hurry, men, get on the boat and take cover inside the cabin."

Before departing for the seaport, Jim and Ben took soundings close to shore. Within ten feet of the beach, the water was only four feet deep. The assault team could wade to the stern of the *Rebecca* without having to use the dinghy. Ben had the cruising boat in position as they arrived. Tilly stood at the stern near the swim ladder to retrieve weapons and help the men aboard.

A loud cry caused Jim to spin around, and he saw young James collapse into the shallow water, his face twisted in pain. He rushed back to assist the fallen resister.

"Sorry, Skipper, guess I twisted my ankle."

Wrapping his arm around the injured man's shoulder, he helped James hobble over to the boat. Tilly and John Phillip reached down, pulled James aboard, and carried him into the cabin. The attacking warriors reached the top of the dune and charged, their bows drawn, shafts of death ready to release.

As Jim climbed over the rail, he yelled through the open door, "Okay Ben, all aboard, take us out of here!"

Arrows zipped like angry wasps, some sticking into the woodwork with a dull thud, others bouncing off the hull. Halfway across the cockpit, Jim tripped and fell onto one knee. As he stood up and glanced back, an arrow plunged into his upper chest. He cried out in agony as he fell backward, landing hard on the fiberglass deck.

Strong hands grabbed his arms and pulled him into the pilothouse. Through the fog of pain, gasping for breath, he heard

Tilly's soothing voice. "Stay with us, Jim, don't you leave us! Hang in there, Skipper."

Moments before he fell off the cliff of consciousness, Jim felt the vibration of the *Rebecca*'s diesel engine as she sped toward the open sea. His last thoughts were of a beautiful doe-eyed girl named Alexa, holding a lantern high above her head with one hand, beckoning with the other. And then, all turned to blackness.

Chapter 44

Blood pooled onto the carpet of the pilothouse. Tilly knelt next to Jim, pressing hard on the wound to slow the bleeding. "John Phillip, I need to pack the wound. Put pressure on each side of the arrow shaft, but try not to move it."

She quickly tore open a package of battle dressings and packed the wound while JT taped it in place. "Is the skipper going to make it, Tilly?"

"We have to stop the bleeding, JT, but it looks like the arrow missed an artery. Let's prop up his feet, so he doesn't go into shock." The young engineer grabbed pillows off a nearby settee to elevate the skipper's legs.

Tilly and John Phillip continued to pile on dressings until the flow of blood slowed to a trickle. Another hour passed until she was satisfied her patient was out of the danger zone.

Leaning over, she whispered into his ear. "Jim, you're going to be okay. Ben and Fredrick are taking us home. We'll be back in Utopia before long."

Exhausted, Tilly sat back, holding her patient's hand, feeling his weak but steady pulse. She'd done all she could for her friend until they returned to the island. His fate now rested in the hands of God.

Hours later, Jim awoke to jolts of pain shooting through the right side of his chest as if someone had poured molten lava into his wound. Through bleary eyes, he imagined seeing a familiar stone fireplace with a boiling kettle on top and a ladle hanging on a hook to one side. He thought this must be a dream because he could've sworn he was back in Timo's cottage.

A beautiful brown face hovered above him. "Well, hello there, Mr. hero of Thormanta," said Tilly with a smile. "Now, you lie still while I examine you." As she checked his dressing, vital signs, and adjusted the I.V., the rescuers gathered around, welcoming their skipper back to the land of the living.

Slurring his words from the pain and drugs, he said, "Hi guys. Guess I became a human pin-cushion. Where are we? Is everyone from the assault team okay?"

JT spoke first. "We're at Timo's place, Skip, and yea, everyone else is okay. You scared the crap out of us for a few hours. Tilly and John Phillip had to do emergency surgery, but you're still with us, and that's all that matters."

Tilly said, "Okay, everyone, visiting hours are over. My patient needs to rest if he's going to make a full recovery. Out you go!"

The crew left with reluctance, passing along words of encouragement. Tilly leaned over and said, "Jim, we leave for the cave in about an hour. The guys are hitching up Galapagos and the wagon to transport you. Rest for now. I'll be back soon." She smiled and squeezed his hand, then walked outside to help the others.

Jim passed out until a lightning bolt of pain jolted him awake, realizing he was in the cart, bouncing along the potholed road leading to the waterfall. Soon, he plunged back into the dark void of unconsciousness.

As night fell, they arrived at the base of the falls, and the men transferred the injured rescuer onto a make-shift stretcher, carrying him up the steep incline. Sentries with flaming torches led the way. The resisters set their patient down at the back of the cavern, covering him with blankets. Tilly woke up Alexa and Catherine to assist her with surgery.

John Phillip left to find Timo and brief him on the mission. Ten minutes later, he returned with a grim look on his face, motioning Ben, JT, and Fredrick to follow him outside.

"Bad news, guys. Timo and four other men are missing. He and three resisters left last night to chase down a man named Benjamin, who they thought might be the traitor. When they didn't show up this morning, Thomas, the senior man, led a search party to follow their trail. Near the stream, they found arrows and spears, but no shell casings. Lots of blood on the ground, but no bodies. I figure Timo and his team walked into a trap and never got off a shot."

They all stared at one another in shock. Fredrick said, "This is indeed tragic news, John Phillip. If there are survivors, they will take them to the dungeons for interrogation. I have heard the horror stories. No one has ever lived through a night of torture in those chambers."

The ex-Navy Seal nodded and continued. "We have to assume the worst, guys. If this Benjamin character is still alive, he'll lead them back to the cave. We need to prepare right away to meet the enemy. I'll pass the word to the head resistance leaders."

Silence settled over the rescuers, realizing how this turn of events changed the tide in favor of the invaders. Once the enemy discovered the location of their hideout, they would hunt them down with a single goal. Total destruction.

THE FINAL BATTLE

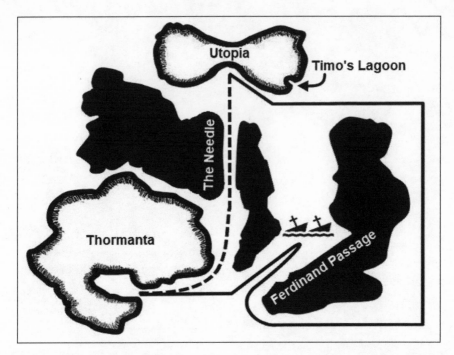

Sailing Routes to Utopia — Roland's route (dashed line) shows the shortcut through The Needle. Tillman's route (solid line) takes longer because of the wrecked longships blocking the Ferdinand Passage. Solid black shaded areas are dangerous coral reefs.

Chapter 45

The tiny gray mouse crawled through a crack at the base of the dungeon door. Making its way over to the severed foot, the creature sniffed at the bleeding wound and putrid fluids oozing onto the cold, cobbled floor.

"Sorry, my little friend," whispered Timo through the blur of throbbing pain, "but today, I have nothing to share. Perhaps, another time?" The mouse wrinkled its nose as it stared back at him, darting away to look for food elsewhere.

Timo shuddered, remembering the tragedy of last night's surprise attack. He wandered into the forest to think about what to do with the traitor Benjamin. Without warning, the enraged cries of the warriors interrupted his prayers as they swarmed like hornets, pouncing on the resisters he'd left behind.

He ran back, but arrived too late. The four bodies of his men lay prone on the cold forest floor, torn to shreds by arrows, spears, and battle axes. In the darkness, the invaders had not recognized their collaborator, Benjamin, his body now among the fallen.

As soon as Timo appeared, the leader of the warrior band recognized him as the head of the resistance group and spared his life, realizing his value in finding the remaining revolutionaries. He would save this one for interrogation in the dungeons.

The invader leader ordered his men to drag the four corpses deep into the woods where they would not be found. Perhaps a search party would assume they had all been captured and come looking for them. More resisters to capture and torture if they could not get this one to talk.

They bound Timo's arms behind his back and marched him four miles to the former grain storage warehouse in town, which now served as a jail. A giant, bare-chested jailer, glistening with sweat, laid Timo on a table, spreading his limbs wide apart. He lashed thick cord to each arm and leg, threading the rope through pulleys, ending at a massive wheel with a hand-crank.

As the muscle-bound jailer tensioned the wheel, the ropes stretched, pulling Timo's arms and legs straight out from the body. The resistance leader screamed as tendons and muscles popped and his joints dislocated. He passed out from the brutal pain, but his captors doused his face with buckets of water to keep him awake.

Opening his eyes, Timo saw a craggy face inches away from his. This man had fiery blue eyes, black shoulder-length hair and a ragged, full beard. Spittle flew as he screamed at Timo, his foul breath like rotted meat. "Talk now, jackal! Speak and you will die a swift death, like your four companions in the forest. Where are you hiding the others? They are not in their homes, so where are they?"

Timo refused to answer. His interrogator, Vlad the Torturer, nodded to the jailer who turned the wheel a full turn. Searing pain shot through Timo's body like a flaming arrow. Each time he came close to losing consciousness, they doused him with water, and another round of torture would begin. But he would not talk.

Filled with fury, Vlad grabbed a battle ax from the wall of the chamber, and severed Timo's left foot in one swift blow, then cauterized the wound with a red-hot poker. The elder resister screamed in agony until he could scream no more, finally passing out.

Vlad gazed down at his prisoner. "Enough for today. Move him to the cell. He's a tough old man, I can say that about him. We do not want to kill him before he tells us the hiding place of his resistance group. We start again at dawn. Get him out of my sight!"

Now, Timo lay on the stone floor of the dungeon, his mind wandering in and out from the shock and pain. As he fell into unconsciousness, he dreamed of a fire-breathing dragon, spitting sheets of flame from its gaping mouth. The resisters fired their rifles into the beast, but the bullets bounced off the monster like stones thrown onto a brick wall.

The animal picked up a woman in its claw, and she disappeared into its fiery mouth. Next, a man succumbed to the clutches of the dragon. Trees caught fire, setting off a series of torches that blocked their escape path.

Timo woke up, crying out as the waves of pain rolled over him. In his heart, he knew the end was near. He felt anger at the world for denying him and his people a chance, at his God for turning away when he needed him most, and at himself for his misdirected rage.

It was not God's fault. This was Timo's burden to bear. He should have marched Benjamin back to the cave to deal with him there. Instead, he opened the door to the specter of death, condemning his men and their prisoner to their fate.

Whispering a prayer through the pain, he said, "God, forgive me for blaming you for my mistake, which brought death to those who trusted me. You gave me free will, and I used it poorly. Take me now before I reveal anything to bring more harm to my friends and neighbors. Show me your mercy, and please, take me now."

His cell door burst open, and two men entered. They pulled the old man up, and he screamed as the stump of his left leg came down hard on the stone surface. The warriors lifted him clear of the floor and carried him down the torch-lit passageway to the chambers. They laid him on the table, spread his arms and legs, then chained them to the rack.

Vlad stood over him, glaring down with hatred at the broken man lying before him. "So, Timo, chieftain of the revolutionaries, you've had plenty of time to consider your fate. What have you decided? Will you tell us the location of your rebels?"

Timo opened his eyes, speaking in a soft voice filled with pain. "You will learn nothing from me. Do with me what you wish, but I will not help you kill more of my people."

Vlad shook his head and shouted in anger, "You old fool. We will not kill you until you tell us what we want to know. No one survives the second day with me without talking. No one!" He turned and nodded to the jailer, who cranked the wooden wheel . . .

The cries of the dying filled the morning with foreboding, scattering a murder of crows from their rooftop perch, high above the chamber of death below.

Chapter 46

The sentry stationed the farthest away sighted the warrior search party, counting twelve men in full battle dress. He signaled the other two guards to pass the word up the line. The man closest to the cave ran back and shouted, "They're coming! At least a dozen invaders, about a mile from us, headed this way. Warn everyone!"

Men grabbed their weapons and ammunition and gathered outside the entrance. John Phillip went over the attack plan one more time. Excited discussions followed the briefing, the men now pumped with adrenaline.

"Okay, quiet down, guys, pipe down. This is what you've been training for, so remember, hold your fire until you have the enemy in your sights. Try to make every round count. Let's do this for Timo and those still missing in action."

The twenty resisters split into two groups. John Phillip and nine men hid behind fallen logs and boulders near the top on each side of the path. The second group, led by Thomas, took cover at the bottom of the incline, hiding behind trees and bushes.

Thomas's men would wait until the warriors passed their position and John Phillip's group opened fire from above. Any invaders still standing would be cut down by a hail of bullets from the rear, trapped in a pincer, with nowhere to run.

A short time later, the Viking war party began a slow ascent up the trail leading to the top of the waterfall. Lying prone behind a fallen log, John Phillip trained his rifle on the forehead of the closest warrior. He held his breath as he squeezed the trigger and fired. The Viking's head exploded in a red cloud. The thunder of gunfire rained death on the warriors, and they fell like dominoes as the bullets found their marks.

As the first shots erupted, the invaders rushed to assist their fallen comrades. Thomas's resisters closed in from behind, firing volleys of steel death. Less than ten minutes later, it was over. Only the leader remained alive. He was a giant of a man with curly blond hair, angry eyes like black marbles, and a full beard.

It took four resisters to restrain the raging prisoner, wrestling him to the ground, where he was gagged and blindfolded. They marched him up the footpath to the cave and placed him in a corner near the back. John Phillip assigned two men to guard the prisoner, then motioned for Tilly to join him outside.

"Tilly, we've captured the head of the pack, but right now, he's madder than a pit bull with an attitude and not talking. Do you have a drug that might help with that? Something to calm him down and open him up, like a truth serum? I want to find out if he knows if Timo and the other missing men are still alive."

She nodded. "Yes, I think I can put something together. Thank God none of the other resisters are hurt. I'll pray for the souls of those who died today, but I cannot understand what's driving their rage? Why do they want to kill innocent men, women and children?"

"Pure hatred and fear, Tilly. They're worried Timo and his people might take back their island." The ex-Navy Seal changed the subject. "So, how's Jim's condition? Still hanging in there?"

"He's much better, and I have the infection under control. I gave him something to help him sleep through the chaos, but he should be awake soon. Well, I better get busy." Tilly hugged him and hurried back to her first-aid station to prepare a truth-cocktail for their captive.

John Phillip sat on a boulder to rest, the blood-rush of a fire-fight now replaced by intense fatigue. Their prisoner held the key to the next move on this chaotic chess board. He wondered if they would finish the mission in time to pass through the black crescent before it shut down for another twenty years. But, then again, what did he have waiting for him back home?

Living alone in a ramshackle house in the Louisiana swamps wasn't exactly the life he'd dreamed about. Here, he'd uncovered his genuine passion, helping the underdog, those less fortunate.

Best of all, the Utopians had genuine love and compassion for one another. A rare find in the postmodern world of the 21st century, where so many folks walked around lost in their phones or earphones, shutting out the human beings surrounding them. That attitude would never cut it here.

Filled with renewed energy, John Phillip strolled back into the cavern, eager to begin the interrogation of the lone survivor.

Chapter 47

"You are doomed—all of you!" shouted the blindfolded prisoner in a slurred voice.

John Phillip grabbed him by his sweat-soaked shoulders, his face inches away. "What happened to the five men who were attacked by your warriors? Are they still alive? Where are you holding them?" The invader's eyes rolled back as Tilly's truth-serum flowed through his veins.

"Only the elder with the long white beard survived. They took him to the dungeons. He refused to talk, so they cut him into pieces, and he bled like a slaughtered lamb. He will be dead by now." Even in his doped-up state, the captured invader managed a grim smile. "No one survives Vlad the Torturer." He closed his eyes, his head bobbing up and down before it dropped to his chest.

Grabbing the prisoner by the hair, John Phillip shouted, "Wake up!" He slapped the invader hard across the face. "What did they learn from the white-bearded man before he died?"

The warrior's eyes opened again, his words now more difficult to understand. "Near the giant waterfall. He would not say where. We were sent to locate your hideout, then return to tell the others. Destroyed your cottages and barns as we marched. Burned everything."

John Phillip tried not to show his shock. He took a deep breath before continuing. "How many warriors are in Utopia?"

The prisoner's voice dropped to a hoarse whisper. "Seventy-five left behind. All the rest in Thormanta for the celebrations. They will come for you. You will face the blades of the dragon warriors." The Viking leader passed out, snoring loudly.

John Phillip turned to Tilly. "Can we keep him awake a few minutes longer?"

"He'll be out until the drugs wear off. Sorry, but I need to step outside for a minute." Tears flowed down her cheeks as Tilly fled from the room into the bright sunshine near the entrance of the cave.

Ben had left the interrogation earlier and was standing outside. He took Tilly in his massive arms as she cried and said, "Oh Ben, Timo's gone." Her body shook with grief.

He hugged her and said, "Look Tilly, we don't know that for sure. This invader might be lying. One way or the other, Timo would want us to be strong. We owe him that."

Tilly gazed into her husband's eyes. "I have to tell Patricia. She and Timo planned to get married when all this was over. She was so happy. I have to tell her about Timo." Ben nodded as his wife walked away to find the elderly woman.

John Phillip knew the news of Timo's capture might cause people to lose their will to fight, which was the last thing he needed to deal with right now. He found the four senior resisters, led them outside the cave to hold an emergency meeting, and told them what the warrior leader had said. As expected, they wanted to take revenge on the prisoner.

Warning them to keep their emotions in check, he said, "This is not the time for revenge, but to prepare to meet the enemy. You can bet that when their scouting party doesn't return, they'll send every warrior left in town to the falls."

Spreading a sketch made earlier on the flat face of a rock, he drew three lines across the incline, dividing it into thirds. "We rig explosives on trip wires here, here and here. We'll set additional devices on the approach to the back side of the cavern. Our captive says there are seventy-five warriors in Utopia. We'll use the same tactics as before, splitting into two groups—one near the top and the other at the base of the hill, everyone hidden behind trees and boulders."

A resister named William asked, "But they will outnumber us almost four to one this time. How can we expect to win a fight against that many battle-hardened warriors?"

The ex-Navy Seal said, "Remember that we have the upper hand because of our superior weapons and explosives. Each man will carry fifty additional bullets. Any of the enemy who makes it past the first resistance group will run into a wire, triggering the grenades. Okay, let's get started."

The leaders returned to the cave to brief the other men while John Phillip walked over to the stack of equipment to prepare the explosives and trip wires. As he worked, he thought about the blood which might flow on both sides of the battle line this time.

Chapter 48

When Jim woke from a deep sleep, Alexa was sitting on the cot with sad eyes, holding his hand next to her cheek. "Hello Jim, how are you feeling? You were in a lot of pain when the men brought you in yesterday."

"Much better, Alexa, thanks for asking." He paused, seeing streaks of tears down her face. "You've heard the news about Timo and the search party?"

She nodded. "All may have been killed except for my father, and he may have died as well. Are they sure about the fate of these other men? Is there hope they too might have been captured?"

"John Phillip interrogated the sole survivor from the skirmish earlier today. This man says Timo was the only one taken to the dungeons. That's all we know, Alexa, but nothing has been confirmed."

She buried her face in her hands and wept. Jim stayed silent, holding her hands, thinking of what Fredrick told him earlier; no one had ever survived the man called Vlad the Torturer. For now, he would keep that to himself and pray for a miracle that his elder friend was still alive.

"Your mother, Alexa? How is she coping with the news?"

Choking back her tears, she said, "The possibility my father perished fills both of us with sorrow, Jim. My mother's strength and resolve helped her overcome her grief after losing her first husband in the massacre of Santa Maria. But now?" Alexa caught her breath, sitting in silence with her eyes closed.

She leaned over and kissed him, her wet cheeks brushing against his face. "I must go be with my mother, darling. I will return soon to check on you, so rest now."

145

Waves of sadness and anger washed over him. Alone now, he pushed himself into a sitting position, working through the thorns and needles of pain as he swung his legs over the cot, planting his feet on the cold cave floor.

"Hey Skipper, what do you think you're doing?" John Phillip halted his stride as he passed by. "You need to rest; so don't you think about getting up. Way too risky, and you might pull Tilly's stitch-work out of those gaping wounds of yours."

"So, John Phillip, I was groggy when you told me about the interrogation. What else did the prisoner say about Timo? Is there a chance he's still alive?"

Speaking in a soft voice, he said, "We have to assume he didn't survive, Skipper. The captive says they hacked off his foot, and he bled to death. Timo never revealed our exact location, just that it was close to the Santa Maria waterfall."

Both men fell silent. Jim's heart pounded in his chest as he tried to imagine the suffering his friend endured. He fought the emotions boiling inside, a combination of hurt and fury.

John Phillip pointed down the passageway. "Right now, we've got our warrior friend trussed up like a Christmas turkey, gagged, blindfolded, and ears plugged. I've assigned two resisters to guard him around the clock. Before he nodded off, he said seventy-five invaders remain in Utopia. I figure we've got about two more days until they send their full force to sniff us out."

He unrolled the sketch in his hand and explained the plan to set multiple traps to snare the enemy as they approached the cave. Jim agreed it was a solid strategy, guaranteed to create chaos in the enemy ranks.

"One more thing, John Phillip, we need to check on the *Rebecca*. Hopefully, the invaders didn't find Timo's hidden cove on their way here. Have the guys run the engine, check the bilges, and make sure the anchor and docking lines are secure."

"Excellent idea, Skip. I'll send Ben and JT to the lagoon right away. Plus, there's a crate of custom-made incendiaries we left aboard. We need those to finish rigging our traps. Get some shut-eye and we'll talk later." The ex-Navy Seal strolled outside to supervise the men preparing for battle.

Jim didn't want to be lying in bed while others fought for their lives. He prayed for God to give him strength, heal his wounds, and help him recover in time to fight the enemy, soon to arrive at the gates of their stone refuge.

Chapter 49

Ben and JT hiked along the forest path, headed for the lagoon to check on Jim's boat. They were quieter than usual after hearing that their elderly friend may have been tortured to death. Ben spoke first. "John Phillip says we're bound to take more casualties when the invaders send the next round of troops. Tilly's gonna have her hands full."

"Got that right, Ben. Still makes me shudder when I think about what happened to the skipper back in Thormanta. Tilly said the arrow missed nicking his heart by a couple of inches. We almost lost him."

Ben held up his hand, signaling JT to stop. He sniffed the air and said, "Smells like burned wood. Someone got here before us, and it wasn't a friendly neighbor.'"

As they crept closer, the charred remains of a chimney appeared. Timo's tiny home was in complete ruins, with a few timbers still standing like the skeletal frame of a mythical beast, blackened and smoldering. The barn, like the cottage, was a burned-out hulk. Galapagos and the two milk cows were nowhere to be found.

Ben took off at a jogger's pace toward the tree line. "Come on JT, let's check on the *Rebecca*." They hurried down the trail to the lagoon. Both men stood speechless on the bank, staring at the cabin cruiser lying on her side like a beached whale. Her starboard hull tilted up at an angle, as if she'd fought, gasping for breath to keep from drowning. The port side was invisible, hidden beneath the surface. The Viking warriors had smashed her pilothouse windows, and jagged edges, like shark's teeth, lined the wooden frames.

Both rescuers stared at one another in shock, realizing this changed everything. Their solitary escape vehicle for leaving Utopia lay in a heap of rubble, broken and beyond repair.

JT whispered in a voice choked with anger. "This ain't good, Ben. Our ride back to Shell Beach and the 21st century just went the way of the freakin' dinosaur."

Ben handed JT his rifle, leaving the combat knife in its sheath strapped to his waist. "We need to find out if John Phillip's explosives are still there. Stay here and keep a lookout while I board the boat."

Muttering a quick prayer, he waded into the chest-high water, making his way to the stern. Using the twisted swim steps for leverage, Ben climbed aboard. Crouching along the inclined deck, he stepped into the pilothouse and descended the ladder to the ruined cabin, wading through the debris of broken glass, rope, chain, and ruptured wood.

He entered the sleeping area near the bow, tossing aside the soggy cushions to access the two plywood frames which formed the support. Pulling off the covers, he reached down into the dark void, touching the sharp corners of the ordnance box. Were the incendiary devices water damaged or still intact?

Ben needed JT's help to lift the heavy box out of the hidden space. He backed out of the compartment, waving to his friend to join him aboard. After propping the rifles against a fallen palm tree, JT jumped into the water and swam out to the trawler.

It took the two men half an hour to wrangle the metal container from the forward cabin up to the deck and move it ashore. Exhausted, they pulled it onto the bank. Ben used a crowbar, salvaged from the pilothouse, to open the sealed lid. Not a drop of water had penetrated inside, and the incendiaries were still in their wrappers, dry as a fishbone. Both men shouted with joy at finding the hidden treasure overlooked by the enemy.

"Well, big guy, now we gotta lug this crate back to John Phillip and tell him and the skipper the rotten news. Don't know about you, but I'm not looking forward to it."

Ben nodded as they slung the rifles on their backs, picked up the box by the handles on each side, and began the long trek back to the cave. Walking in silence, the two rescuers realized they were now stuck in the twilight-zone of the 19th century, and this time there'd be no escape back to the future.

Chapter 50

The rustle of bushes nearby caused Ben and JT to dive for the ground. They pulled the box of explosives behind a stump. How had the invaders sneaked up on them without warning? Twigs snapped as the intruders closed in. With their fingers on the trigger of their rifles, both men whipped around ready to blast away.

Instead, they stared in shock at the gray face of a four-legged beast standing six feet from the rescuers, her eyes blinking in surprise. "Honk. Honk-honk." Galapagos, Timo's friendly mule, greeted them in the usual manner.

JT shouted, "Dang, Galapagos, you crazy dummy, we almost shot you! Where in tarnation did you come from? We thought you were charcoal briquettes or mule jerky. Nice to see you again, old girl." He smiled as he patted the animal's snout.

Ben shook with laughter until his eyes teared up. "Well, well, JT, our transportation has arrived, and praise God for that. It'll be a lot easier than lugging fifty pounds of ordinance four more miles. Tell you what, you and Galapagos wait here. I'll go back to the boat to find what we need to rig a saddle and harness."

Returning to the wreckage, Ben loaded blankets, rope, and extra bags into a plastic storage container and floated the gear ashore. He and JT rigged a makeshift cushion to the mule. Next, they divided the explosives into even piles, stuffing them into the canvas pouches. Hanging them on each side of the hefty animal helped balance the weight.

Before leaving, the two men filled the empty, oblong weapons container with rocks, sinking it to the bottom of the lagoon to hide evidence from the enemy.

Two hours later, near sunset, they arrived back at the cavern. John Phillip met them at the entrance. He laughed at their mode of transportation. "Well, what do we have here? Nice to see the furry beast again guys, but we can't keep her at the cave. Maybe a resister owns a farm nearby where she can stay. Okay, let's hear your story."

JT and Ben glanced at one another, each taking a deep breath as they took turns relating the story of Timo's cottage burned to the ground, and the skipper's cabin cruiser sunken and beyond repair. The ex-Navy Seal's mouth dropped open as he listened to their tale.

"No dang way, little bro! They sank Jim's boat, our only way off this island?" He slammed his fist on a bag in anger, gazing out over the valley, lost in thought for several minutes.

John Phillip turned and said, "Okay guys, let's stay focused. We made promises to these folks when we offered to stay and help. Let's do this, for the skipper, for Timo, for the Utopians. Finish the mission. Sound like a plan?" Both men nodded without hesitation.

"Ben, you break it to Tilly. JT and I will be with Jim."

Ben found Tilly inside the cave, talking with Patricia. He waved her over, walking outside into the cool evening breeze.

She cried out in disbelief. "Oh no, darling, not Jim's boat! Oh, my God, this means . . ." She stopped for a moment as her eyes glistened with tears. "Does this mean we'll never return to our home in Shell Beach again?"

He took her in his arms. "Right now, Till, only God has that answer. We are not alone here, but with people we love and new friends like Catherine, Patricia, Alexa, and Fredrick. I figure God put us here for a purpose, and we need to trust Him. He gave you a second chance with Timo's tea and that alone is a miracle."

Tilly, as always, quickly recovered from her shock, realizing her man had nailed it on the head. She smiled, wiped her eyes and said, "Has anyone broken the news to Jim yet?"

"John Phillip and JT are telling him now. He's a strong one, the skipper is, but he loved his boat. Lived aboard her the past four years."

Tilly hugged her husband, holding him tight, feeling the slight movement inside her belly, the first signs of a child soon to be born. They joined the others at the foot of Jim's cot.

To say the skipper was angry was an understatement. He wasn't mad at them, but at himself for putting his rescuers in harm's way. And now this? In a voice choked with sadness, he said, "Guys, thanks for leveling with me, but I'd like to be alone for a while."

John Phillip nodded for everyone to leave. As soon as the room cleared, he said, "Jim, I don't know what you're thinking, but if you're looking for someone to chat with, I'm your man. I'll be right around the corner. Holler if you need anything."

For the next half hour, Jim thought of alternate scenarios; most made no sense at all, until, out of nowhere, his brain lit up like a light bulb with a possibility that might work. He yelled for the ex-Navy Seal, asking him to locate Fredrick.

Five minutes later, they returned, and the blond sailor asked, "Jim, I am sorry to learn of the loss of your fine ship. How can I help?"

"Thanks, I believe you can. The *Rebecca*'s not the only boat available. How many ships did the chieftains leave back in Utopia when they sailed for Thormanta?"

"Two longships, each about sixty feet long, Jim. One vessel, called *Raven*, has a fracture in the hull and needs repair, but the other, the *Falcon Crest*, is ready for sea. I have sailed aboard her, and she is a fine vessel, quite easy for a small crew to handle."

Jim's vision was simplicity itself. After defeating the enemy, they would seize one of the Viking ships, sail it back through the black crescent, and find their way home.

Chapter 51

White pockets of mist rose from the floor of the valley as the late morning sun peaked over the hilltops. The lookout spotted a dark, wavy line moving beneath the haze. He peered through binoculars to get a better look, and fear surged through his veins as he sighted the shields and spears of the approaching war party. Pulling his signal mirror from his coat pocket, he flashed the warning signal to the other sentinel, stationed on a distant cliff near the falls . . .

JT rushed into the cave and found his brother next to Jim's cot. "Here they come! Enemy troops inbound, less than three miles away. Lookout counts at least sixty, maybe more."

John Phillip glanced at the skipper and said, "A lot sooner than we thought, Jim. We won't have time to rig all the incendiaries, but we've set enough trip wires to do plenty of damage."

He turned to his younger brother. "JT, warn the others to take their positions. Let's give our friends a welcoming they won't forget."

The cave erupted in a beehive of activity as the men checked and rechecked their rifles and strapped on combat knives. Ben passed out spare ammo. Each of the twenty men received fifty extra rounds. All total, the defenders had over 1,000 steel darts of death to throw against the enemy when they arrived.

Jim convinced Tilly he was strong enough to hobble around on make-shift crutches the men had put together with branches and twine. He would guard the front entrance to the cavern while the elders defended the opening at the rear.

Fredrick joined Ben, JT, and John Phillip outside. Catherine, Alexa, and Patricia helped Tilly prepare the makeshift first-aid station for casualties. They organized battle dressings, antibiotics, scalpels, sutures, I.V. stands, heart monitors, and razor-sharp saws for battle wounds requiring amputation.

As he sat in a chair near the cave entrance, Jim recalled Tilly telling him about a week-long training exercise she attended in the remote Florida Everglades. The physician in charge taught techniques gleaned from his time as a medic on the battlefields of Iraq and Afghanistan.

Mockups included lifelike mannequins with broken necks, crushed legs, arms, and backs, and gaping wounds, some with severed arteries gushing blood like a fire hose. With no hospitals nearby, they set up their own tents, latrines, and surgical centers. No amenities included in this vacation package.

Tilly said she learned more in a week about survival in brutal conditions than she could've learned in a year of advanced nursing school. So here, in her spare time, she passed along those skills to the other Utopian women. Her medical team gathered in the tiny space, holding hands as they prayed for those defending their home.

The first explosion sounded like a thunderclap, and two more followed in quick succession. Limping over to the front of the cave, Jim sighted the smoke in the distance. The sounds of men in combat echoed off the cave walls. Gunfire erupted as the resisters fired their volleys into the enemy, catching them by surprise.

Two invaders found their way to the entrance. Jim squinted down the barrel, waiting until the last minute to fire two bullets into the chest of the first warrior. He crumpled to the ground, a stunned expression on his face. His enraged companion rushed forward with a gleaming double-edged battle ax held overhead. Two rounds to the head and one to the chest blew him off his feet. He fell in a heap twenty feet away.

The noise of the raging battle was deafening. Another warrior broke through, rushing toward the opening to the cavern, taking cover behind a boulder. Jim shifted his position, expecting him to rush from the right, but the man disappeared from sight.

Seconds later, a resister named Peter surprised the crouching invader from behind, dispatching him with his combat knife. He waved to Jim as he rose above the rocky outcrop, giving him a thumbs up. His blood-covered blade revealed the rest of the story.

An hour after it had begun, the sounds of gunfire dwindled to a sporadic pop, pop, pop, like firecrackers in the distance. Soon, quiet settled over the battlefield, littered with the fallen, the only sound coming from the cascading waterfall.

John Phillip, Ben, JT, and Fredrick returned to the cave, weary but in high spirits. "It was a quick one this time, Skip," said John Phillip. "We count seventy-three dead and another two who won't make it. Our casualties are three minor scrapes and one slight cut."

Jim couldn't believe it was over, at least for this island. They cheered for their victory, believing the people of Utopia could now live in peace and freedom. Unknown to anyone that day, their fight for survival was far from over.

Chapter 52

The eight ships destroyed in the Thormantan seaport were not the only sea-going war wagons available. Even Fredrick did not know about the secret shipyard, hidden away on the remote west coast of the invader's island home.

Five massive Viking longships, each 120 feet long, were preparing for the invasion of Utopia. The fire-breathing dragons of Jim's nightmares would soon unleash their fury upon the unsuspecting resisters and rescuers.

Tillman the Great, ruling chieftain of Thormanta, seethed with anger as he watched the master shipbuilder, Francisco, inspect the rigging on one of the giant ships. "These rebels believe they can stop us by burning our seaport?" He scoffed and said, "Finish your sea trials by early afternoon, shipwright, for we sail with the tide tonight. I will turn the island of Utopia into a river of blood!"

Each vessel underwent an extensive on-the-water test to check the integrity of her rowing, steering and sailing ability. Four of the ships passed these rigorous tests and had been delivered to the port earlier. But this one was far from ready.

Francisco shook his head. "She will not be fit for sea if we rush, chieftain. This vessel needs new blocks and backing plates for the rigging which supports her mast. She will be ready tomorrow afternoon at the earliest, but no sooner."

The warrior leader glared back in anger. "I will listen to none of your excuses! Deliver the last ship to the harbor before the sun sets. If you cannot complete the task, find someone who can. We set sail at midnight. No delays!" Tillman stomped off in a huff, leaving the boat builder speechless.

"What a fool," said the shipwright to himself. "You know nothing about a ship's requirements to handle the demands of Aegir, god of the sea. All you live for is to kill and plunder the weak and helpless. A conqueror, nothing more."

Francisco spat on the ground in disgust, turned, and walked back to the forge to talk with his blacksmith. They would have to use older, weaker spare parts to rig the ship within the demanded time frame. If the man wanted inferior rigging, so be it.

Endangering a ship's crew was not the way of a true sea captain. The souls of the warriors manning the defective ship now rested in the hands of this half-crazed chieftain. He shook off the dark thoughts of what might happen on the journey.

Later that day, Tillman gathered his council of chieftains in the empty chambers of the great banquet hall. Their talk focused on spilling the blood of the traitor Fredrick and removing the rebellious Utopians from the face of the earth.

The head chieftain's voice rose to a crescendo. "Tonight, we sail for Utopia to take revenge on the islanders who attacked our harbor, burned our dragon ships, and destroyed our supply warehouses. The warriors who chased after them reported they escaped on a fast ship which maneuvers without oars or sail. How they learned to build such a vessel, I do not know, but that is of no concern to me. In a few hours, our five greatest longships depart for the shores of our enemy. These insurgents will soon feel the Thormantan hammers of 300 mighty warriors, who will crush them like bugs underfoot. Long ago, our ancestors believed they finished off the resisters at Santa Maria, but they failed. To honor them, we will complete this task once and for all. Before the end of the week, my brethren, victory will be ours!"

The group cheered as they whipped out their daggers, drumming the butts of the knives on the table in a deafening frenzy. Tillman lifted his gigantic arms overhead, hands clasped, as the shouts of the bloodthirsty mob echoed through the chamber halls. His brethren electrified him, and he imagined himself immortal, omnipotent, soon to become a legendary warrior-god of Norse poems and sagas, his fame assured for centuries to come.

The young shipyard worker with short, curly brown hair strolled past the banquet hall toward the smoldering ruins of the seaport. The madness of the crowd inside sounded like rolling thunder in the otherwise peaceful afternoon.

Raised as a sailor, now an apprentice rigger, Roland had just learned of the chieftain's plans and wondered what he could do. His boyhood friend Fredrick a traitor? In Roland's eyes, he was a hero, like those in the legends of the Norse poets.

He thought back to their younger years when the two boys spent long days together, running along the white-sand beaches, swimming in the harbor, fishing off the docks, or watching the warriors practice swordsmanship in town.

Stolen at birth from their Utopian mothers, the boys were forced to learn the ways of warfare. Neither young man ever put these skills into practice. Roland had recurring dreams where his mother would appear to comfort him, begging him to live a life of peace. Fredrick described a similar vision which came to him late at night. Soon after, they promised one another to follow the advice of their spirit mothers. Roland became a ship's rigger and Fredrick a sailmaker.

But now, his lifelong friend and the peaceful people of Utopia were in mortal danger. How could he warn the islanders of the hellfire about to be unleashed upon them?

Chapter 53

Three armed men huddled in the late afternoon shadows of the abandoned grain storage building. The tall, husky blond man peered around the corner, expecting guards at the entrance to the torture chambers, but all appeared deserted. He signaled for the others to wait, crouched, and ran to the open doorway, stepping over the threshold into the den of death . . .

After the skirmish, Jim and John Phillip believed the town would be safe to search for Timo and the other missing resisters. They appointed Fredrick to lead the search party.

In his heart, Fredrick doubted anyone was still alive, but he would not leave until he inspected every cell and chamber.

Torches flickered on the shadowy walls of the dungeons as he descended the winding stone stairwell leading to the bowels of the prison. He listened for sounds of suffering, but all was quiet; the stench of death and decay everywhere.

The torture rooms were empty, with black, dried blood dripped or splotched on the racks, table, and floors, but no sign of life. Next, he searched the tiny cells lining each side of the passageway, finding only skulls, bones, and decomposing bodies.

On his way out, he passed a small room he had missed the first time, hidden out of view below the stone steps. The interior, bathed in shadows, appeared unoccupied. As he was about to ascend the steps, a faint whisper broke through the stillness.

Fredrick hesitated to enter the cell, fearing the ghosts of the dead, who, it was said, wandered these chambers of horror forever. But this whisper became more distinct. "Wait. Please wait."

Were his ears playing tricks on him? He peered into the tiny cell, seeing only a bundle of soiled rags piled in a far corner. Fredrick jumped back when he saw the mound of cloth move, and a groaning noise came from under the pile. Approaching with caution, he reached down, touching the cold, naked body of a man beneath the rags. Taking a deep breath, he rolled the bundle over, gasping as he recognized the familiar face.

Timo's eyes winced in pain as he cried out, shivering, the bloody, ragged stump of his leg seeping blood, putrid with infection. Fredrick made a dressing from strips of rags, but liquid continued to pour from the severed limb. He pressed more rags over the wound, lashing them with a length of rope, tying a second rope above the knee as a tourniquet. Within minutes, the flow of blood slowed to a trickle.

Covering the elder resistance leader with his coat, he whispered, "Timo, it is Fredrick. Catherine and Alexa are waiting for you back at the cave. Stay strong, my friend. I will return soon to take you home."

He charged up the steps of the prison, burst into the sunlight, telling the two resisters the splendid news. "Come quick, I've found Timo. He is alive, but close to death."

They returned to the chambers, gathering poles, ropes, and blankets from other rooms to form a makeshift stretcher. Strapping their injured leader to the litter, the men made the long journey back to the cave, arriving late in the night. Timo was barely alive, his breathing erratic.

Fredrick shook Tilly awake. "Tilly, we have returned with Timo, but he has terrible wounds and hovers near death." As she was putting on her coat, he described the infected, missing limb and other injuries.

Tilly told the young blond sailor to wake the other women on her medical team. "Also, I need you to boil a pot of water. We'll need that right away for surgery. Hurry, Fredrick, please hurry."

He found Catherine and told her the news. She hugged and kissed him and went back to tell the two women, and their cries of happiness echoed throughout the cavern. Alexa and Patricia embraced Fredrick, crying tears of joy. He gently broke away and said, "Go now, Tilly needs your help." All three women rushed to the back of the cave.

Fredrick filled an iron pot with water and placed it on the fire. Overwhelmed with fatigue, he sat on a nearby boulder to wait. Gazing up into the star-filled sky, he whispered a prayer. "God, if you are listening, please help these women save this brave elder tonight. He is so near death, I do not see hope for him, but perhaps you do."

Seconds later, a cluster of shooting stars streaked across the heavens, yellowish-white light bursting in a shower of sparks, like a flint drawn across a bar of steel. Another group of the tiny lights followed the first. Was this a sign from Catherine's God, an answer to his prayer? He must ask her more about this later.

The sound of soft bubbles bursting on the surface of the boiling water interrupted his thoughts. Picking up the heavy, steaming pot, Fredrick hurried back to Tilly and her surgical team, now fighting to save the life of the beloved leader of the Utopians.

Chapter 54

The tiny sailboat with the square sail raced over the bumpy seas with a fair wind astern. An umbrella of twinkling stars and a quarter-moon reminded Roland how much he missed the beauty of the ocean. But tonight was not the time to relax. He must journey to the island of Utopia to warn his friend of the looming invasion.

When he was younger, Roland would sit for hours, listening to the sea tales of the elders. There was a narrow passage to the north called the Needle, which saved many hours, but the longships dared not enter because of the shallow water and coral reefs. The senior sailors said a small sailboat might make it through, with luck and a blessing from Aegir, god of the sea.

Tonight, the winds blew from the south, and a crystal clear horizon greeted him. Roland planned to sail along the eastern shore of Thormanta, then turn north to the notorious Needle. He would shoot through the shallow channel and enter the open sea on the other side. This should keep him clear of the war fleet, scheduled to depart in a few hours. The longships would have to use the Ferdinand Passage, a much longer but safer route.

Fear and doubt crept over him, his thoughts firing like thunderbolts inside his brain. "I've risked everything to do this, and I'll never be able to return to Thormanta. If I crash into the razor-sharp reefs, I will drown. If the ships catch up with me, they will torture and hang me. I have no choice but to keep going."

He rounded the eastern point of the island and settled onto the four-mile stretch of open ocean, using Polaris, the North Star, to steer a steady course. The winds increased as his boat skipped like a flat stone over the small waves.

Less than an hour later, Roland sighted the frothing white water which marked the position of the deadly reefs. Now he had to locate the slender passage to lead him between the ship-killing underwater coral heads into the pass.

He recalled the advice of one older sailor who made this treacherous journey in a small sailing skiff years ago. "First, you must find the gateway into the channel, then steer your boat between two coral reefs so close you can reach out and touch them! One mistake and your vessel turns to kindling wood!"

Roland strained his eyes to find the opening, but nothing appeared except a line of breakers. He sailed back and forth along the southern edge, peering into the passage, looking for any sign of an entrance.

A few minutes later, the moon broke through a cloud, casting beams of light onto the sea, and he sighted a sliver of a channel, which appeared as narrow as a worn forest path. Grabbing the sheet, he pulled in his sail and steered toward the entry point.

Holding his breath, he threaded the boat through the eye of the narrow Needle. A coral head scraped the port side, but the sailboat kept going at top speed. Now, three miles of dangerous channel remained until he cleared the pass.

The old salt's words of long ago played over and over in his brain, and indeed, the shoals appeared close enough to touch. Breakers hissed like a nest of vipers, only an arm's length away. Without moonlight, passage would be impossible, and he thanked the gods for lighting the path.

Another rocky reef struck the right side of his vessel, and she jerked to a halt. He tugged hard on the tiller, but the little ship would not respond. At the last moment, the sailboat heeled hard, bounced off the reef, and continued on her way.

However, Roland's troubles were far from over. A foot-long gash appeared along the starboard hull, three inches above the waterline; its jagged edges gaped back at him like a shark's open mouth. If the vessel heeled too far over, she might flood and sink.

Once he sailed into open water again, he would need to make repairs to his wounded boat to keep her afloat. A mile ahead, Roland spotted the far end of the Needle, but the path appeared blocked by frothing white breakers, warning him of more coral to come. Was there no opening?

His heart filled with fear and his mind with dark thoughts. "Am I now trapped forever in a three-sided wall of rocky death, with only one entrance, which now lies behind me? I have no room to turn around, so I must keep going, and may the gods protect me from destruction."

Roland gripped the tiller with all his strength to hold his damaged ship in the center of the channel. As he closed in on the deadly coral reefs ahead, he shut his eyes and braced for the crushing impact which was sure to come. Moments later, a mountainous wave from behind lifted the stern high into the air and the tiny ship cartwheeled.

The young sailor tumbled forward, striking his head on the wood-planked cockpit floor. His last conscious thought was of falling head over heels into the turbulent sea, surrounded by a blackness darker than the night.

Chapter 55

Five warships carrying sixty men each, loaded with weapons and provisions, set sail from Thormanta at midnight. Winds from the southwest filled their sails as they sped to the east toward the Ferdinand Passage.

Tillman intended to lead the fleet in his flagship, *Red Dragon*, but a rip in the sail caused his ship to fall behind. By the time the sailmaker repaired the torn seam, his vessel was in the middle of the pack. They would need to wait until they cleared the dangerous reefs to move to the head of the line.

Now, he stood near the bow, feeling his ship's power as she sliced through the waves with the grace of a dolphin. He sighted the two longships in the lead entering the passage. Minutes later, the first ship disappeared from view as if pulled underwater by the gods.

Tillman yelled back to the ship's master. "Captain, where is the lead vessel?"

Sven assigned a senior sailor to take over the steering, then dashed forward to join the chieftain at the bow. He shuddered as he realized what happened. "She has lost her mast and struck the coral reefs! They are doomed!"

As predicted by the shipwright Francisco, the wrecked longship's rigging snapped from the strain of her wind-filled sail. Without adequate support, the mast toppled over like a falling tree.

Within seconds, the second warship following close behind collided with the stranded vessel, its bow crushed inward like an eggshell. The ship tilted over at a sickening angle, spilling men into the sea. Now two massive longships lay in ruins, blocking the entire width of the narrow channel.

"We cannot proceed further, Chieftain!" Turning to the closest oarsman, he shouted, "Blow the alarm to warn the two ships behind us. We must turn around now before we crash into the wrecks!"

The sailor grabbed the carved goat's horn and blew the danger signal to alert the vessels astern. The captains on the two other longships heeded the alarm, changing course to head back to the entrance and out into safe water.

Sven returned to the steering station. To avoid colliding with the ships astern, he had to wait for the other vessels to finish turning. He prayed to the gods for them to hurry. With only half a mile to go, his prayers were answered. The captain pulled the massive tiller to one side, and the mighty vessel turned and headed back out the channel.

As they sailed to the south, the screams of the drowning sailors carried over the wind, loud at first, but growing fainter with time, until all was quiet except for the roar of the breakers of the passage.

Sven rejoined the warrior chieftain at the bow. "As soon as we are clear of the reefs, we can douse sail and row back to rescue those still alive. We cannot leave our comrades to be eaten by the giant gray sharks, Chieftain. Those men are our friends and neighbors and . . ."

Before he could finish, Tillman interrupted. "Silence! I'm in charge here, Captain, and we do not stop until we reach the island of our enemy. Control your emotions, or I will relieve you of your command."

The ferocity of the warrior leader's response shocked Sven into silence. His mind filled with ghastly images of the devilish sharks, gorging on the flesh of the fallen. By dawn, the waters of the Ferdinand Passage would turn blood-red as the rising sun.

Tonight, Tillman had revealed himself to be a monster; a man without a conscience. How many more warriors would he be willing to sacrifice in his quest for glory?

"So, tell me, Captain, how much time will this alternate route add to our journey?" The chieftain's question jolted Sven from his black thoughts.

"Six to eight hours. Once we enter the open sea, we will sail east along the southern rim of the reefs. When we turn north, fair winds will fill our sails for a swift passage to the island."

Tillman stood on a rower's bench near the bow of the *Red Dragon* as he spoke to the crew, his baritone voice booming above the wind and sea. "Men, we lost many noble warriors tonight. Remember why you are here—to crush those who dare to oppose us in Utopia. Those who died tonight ascend to Valhalla. You must honor their sacrifices with a mighty victory. Are you ready to become the newest heroes of the sagas of Thormanta? Do you accept the challenge before you?"

His speech, as in the great hall of the chieftains, roused the men from their depressed thoughts. Many cheered and shouted their allegiance to the head chieftain and their ancestors.

But there were those among the crew who remained silent, horrified by their ruler's lack of compassion. This madman could have turned around to rescue the shipwrecked sailors fighting for their lives. Instead, he sailed on. This night they would never forget, and this man, they would never forgive.

Chapter 56

The damaged sailboat bobbed up and down in the gentle Gulf swell. Her broken mast floated near the hull, held alongside by long lengths of heavy rope. Thunk, thunk, thunk.

The banging sound woke Roland, and he opened his eyes, squinting in the bright sunlight. Pain surged through his body from his fall, and he felt dried blood caked on his forehead.

Glancing astern, he sighted the foaming white water of the Needle about two miles to the south. He recalled the rogue wave which lifted the stern of his tiny ship over the coral heads, and he thanked Aegir, the sea-god, for sparing him.

Now he needed to cut away the torn sail and tangled rigging to free the mast before it punched a hole in the boat and the vessel sank. He found the small ax he'd packed in his bag before departing. Lifting the cutting tool high overhead, he brought the sharp blade down onto the ropes, severing the tentacles one after another.

He continued to chip away at the binding ropes for another hour until, at last, the timber floated free. Next, he used remnants of the ripped sail to repair the gash in the hull, sliced open by the coral heads during his passage. Exhausted from his labors, he sat back to catch his breath. To the north, the faint outline of Utopia peaked above the distant horizon.

No more time for idle rest; I must keep going if I am to survive, he thought, as he slid the oars into the square oarlocks, lashed the tiller, and pointed the bow toward the island.

As he rowed, Roland watched for signs of the war fleet. At any moment, they might appear. Those colossal longships sailed much faster than his tiny, broken sailboat. Would he arrive at the port before they caught up with him?

When his boat tumbled over the wave, his water jug fell overboard. His parched, swollen tongue stuck to the roof of his mouth, but he dared not drink the sea water. The elders told tales of shipwrecked sailors, scooping the salty liquid into their bellies, only to vomit until they died a violent death of dehydration.

With each stroke of the wooden oars, his strength ebbed like a falling tide. The merciless rays of the sun scorched his bare head; sweat poured down his face into his eyes, blurring his vision.

In his weariness, he imagined seeing a tall man in a tattered white robe emerge from the tiny cabin of his sailboat. At first, Roland was terrified, but soon a calm came over him, a feeling of peace, hard to define. Shaking his head, he looked again, but the ghostly image had vanished. Was his mind playing tricks on him?

As he bent forward again to pull on the oars, both of his arms cramped, and he cried out in anguish, dropping to the deck on his knees. Burning pain, like the red-hot tongs of a blacksmith, surged through his body from his shoulders to his fingertips.

Unable to move, he stayed buckled over until, a short time later, a cool touch caused him to raise his head. The man from before was sitting on the bench seat beside him, one hand resting on his shoulder.

"Roland, do not be afraid, for I am here with you, as I have always been, and always will be. Rest now, and when you awake, you will continue on your journey."

Roland fell into a deep sleep until a playful wave sprayed his face, startling him. He checked the cabin and scanned the sea all around, but the man who had talked to him had disappeared. For some mysterious reason, the painful cramps were gone, his thirst a distant memory, his energy restored.

Grabbing the oars, Roland propelled his tiny ship swiftly through the calm waves. Within the hour, he passed between the two headlands marking the entrance to the Utopian port. As he glanced astern, three black dots emerged on the southern horizon, their square sails billowing in the fresh breeze. The Thormantan battle fleet had arrived.

Digging his oar blades deeper into the blue-green water of the harbor, Roland pulled with all his might, now in a life-or-death race against time.

Chapter 57

Through the fog of pain, Timo heard female voices, and thought, "The music of the angels, so I must be in heaven." No matter how hard he tried, he could not open his eyes. He groaned in frustration and despair.

A soothing voice whispered in his ear. "Dear, it's Patricia. I'm here, and you are safe, back in the cave. Fredrick found you and brought you here." Gentle hands touched his shoulders, and a soft kiss, like the wings of a butterfly, tickled his forehead. Timo struggled to answer, but his lips failed to respond.

Another gentle voice above him said, "Well, hello, Timo. Tilly here, and you're going to be okay. I need to find out how much pain you are in right now. So, on a scale of one to ten, squeeze my hand with the highest number, which defines the level of your discomfort."

She counted five squeezes and adjusted the I.V. fluid flow rate. "Okay, thanks, Timo. Rest for now, and I'll be back soon to check on you."

Moments later, Patricia whispered, "Alexa and I will be here when you wake up, dear. Go back to sleep." More butterfly kisses brushed his cheeks. He dreamed of a bright day in a field of white and yellow daisies, he and his love chasing one another like children at play.

Bone tired from four hours in surgery, Tilly stepped out into the late morning sunlight to join her husband. He took her in his arms, holding her in silence, feeling the beat of her heart.

"What kind of hatred would drive a human being to do this to another person, Ben?" She paused, then continued. "He's out of danger, but we had to remove the left leg above the knee. I hope we've stopped the spread of infection, but only time will tell."

Ben grimaced and shook his head. "You've done all you can, Till. Let's leave the rest in God's hands. Timo's a fighter, just like the Skipper, and he'll pull through, you'll see."

After checking on the senior resistance leader, the remaining rescuers walked outside the cave to join their friends. They hugged Tilly, thanking her for bringing their elder friend back from the edge of death's door.

Tilly smiled and said, "Thanks, everyone, but this was a gift from God, and a miracle that Fredrick was able to find him in time. A few more hours and Timo wouldn't have survived."

"And speaking of our blond friend," said Jim, "I've sent him and two other resisters, along with Timo's mule and cart, back into town for more supplies. While we're together, there's one more thing. We're in a time crunch to pass through the crescent. While Fredrick's in town, he'll find us a sailing ship. My plans are to drop you off at Shell Beach, and return to Utopia. This place is like home to me."

Ben grabbed Tilly's hand and spoke first. "Skip, Tilly and I talked long and hard. We might end up stuck here, but that wouldn't be so bad. Tilly is free of her cancer, far as we can tell. We stay, she lives. If we go back, well, the docs have already said they're out of ideas. So, we're staying."

John Phillip looked over at JT. Both brothers nodded to one another. "Me and my little bro have talked it over, too, Skip. Something's crazy about this place and the people here, like they kinda grow on you. Besides, we've always daydreamed about having our own farm, and this location is just about perfect."

Jim was stunned, expecting his crew to be eager to return to the life they left. There was indeed a strange magic about this tropical island paradise. Something mystical beyond explanation. He thanked everyone for sharing their thoughts, turned and limped back inside the cavern to check on his elder friend.

Patricia and Alexa knelt near Timo's cot, holding hands, their heads bowed in prayer. He gazed upon both women, awed by their beauty, strength, love, and compassion. And, at that moment, he realized why his crew wanted to remain on this island on the far side of the black crescent.

For here, life was about the other person, not about the self. Jim limped back to his cot to get some rest. He soon fell into a deep sleep, but this time, there were no nightmares of death by dragons or drowning.

Chapter 58

The sniper peered over the rooftop, spotting the small sailboat entering the harbor from the sea, its mast broken off to a small stump, the rigging a mess of ropes lashed to the deck. The rower wore a turban-like headband with a flap over the neck to ward off the scorching heat of the mid-morning sun.

When they arrived in the abandoned town, Fredrick assigned Solomon to the roof of the old grain warehouse to watch for threats while they loaded Timo's wagon with food and blankets to take back to the cave.

The young, black-haired Utopian prided himself on his abilities with the new weapons the rescuers brought to the island. During practice, the stranger from another land named John Phillip complimented Solomon on his ability to hit the targets every time in quick succession. In the skirmish the day before, he fired only ten bullets, and nine found their mark.

A single bullet to the head of the man rowing the broken sailboat and one more enemy would cease to exist. He would like nothing more than to turn the white turban in his sights to bright red, but he recalled Fredrick's command. "No one must find out we are here, Solomon. If you see anyone, come and warn us right away. Do not fire your weapon except in a life-threatening circumstance."

With hesitation, he eased his index finger off the trigger. No matter his personal feelings, he would not risk the lives of his companions. He hurried down the stone steps to the street, jogging to the building two doors away to alert his friends about the lone intruder.

Roland rowed his boat the final half mile, attached the docking lines, and climbed the ladder to the top of the wood-planked wharf. Fatigue hit him like an avalanche. Spotting a water barrel, he doused his head with the cool liquid, scooping more into his mouth. Still dizzy from dehydration, he sat with his back against the barrel, facing seaward.

The three dots appeared larger now, with square-shaped, well-defined sails. The longships would enter the port in less than an hour. But where was the rest of the invader fleet? There should be five warships approaching Utopia. With no more time to contemplate, he pushed himself to his feet, and for the first time noted the emptiness of the streets and buildings. The port town appeared abandoned, with no signs of life.

Three men stepped into the street from the warehouse across from the wharf. He recognized his childhood friend and companion Fredrick right away by his stocky build and long, blond locks. He cried out, "Fredrick, it is I, Roland!"

Fredrick and his two companions raised their rifles, aiming at the stranger. "You there! Stop or we will shoot. Put your hands in the air!"

Raising his hands high in a gesture of surrender, the bearded man said, "Fredrick, I am your friend, Roland, here to warn you of the coming invasion of the raiders of Thormanta." He pointed to the south.

Peering through Jim's binoculars, Fredrick counted three gigantic warships closing in fast. Confusion and doubt set in. Where had they come from? He had witnessed the eight moored Thormantan ships burned to ash with his own eyes. And now this?

He ran over to the man, spun him around and gasped as he recognized the face and distinct curly brown hair. "Roland! It is you!" He embraced his best friend from childhood, looking at the tiny sailboat with her broken mast, tied up next to the wharf. "You sailed all the way here in this small craft? How did you lose your mast? Tell me what happened."

Roland related the story of his perilous journey from Thormanta through the coral reefs in The Needle, the capsizing and breaking his mast, and finally rowing the last four miles with the war fleet close behind.

Fredrick shook his head in disbelief. "But this makes no sense. We destroyed all the invaders' longships back in Thormanta. So, where did this fleet of dragon ships on the horizon come from?"

Roland explained. "Only the head chieftains know of this secret shipyard on the western shore of Thormanta. There, they built full-sized longships over one-hundred-feet long, each capable of carrying sixty warriors. The only reason I found out was from working on the rigging before they were delivered to the port to prepare for the invasion."

He paused as he looked out toward the inbound war ships. "I believe all five vessels set sail, but sighted only three on my way here. Perhaps the other two longships ran into difficulty. This, I do not know."

Fredrick signaled his men to lower their weapons and embraced his boyhood friend again. "Thank you for risking your life to warn us, Roland. We must hurry to alert the others in our hideout. Come, we have no time to waste."

The men finished packing the supplies into the cart and headed back to the cave. They realized what this meant; the earlier skirmish was only a warm-up exercise. The ultimate battle to determine the fate of Utopia was about to begin.

Chapter 59

The rescuers gathered near the entrance to the cavern, passed out weapons and ammo, and listened to Roland's story. The news was chilling. Five full-size longships with sixty men each departed the previous evening. Three hundred battle-hardened warriors would soon be headed their way.

John Phillip held a quick meeting to assign tasks and prepare for an assault. He picked four men to help him rig booby traps with the incendiaries that Ben and JT recovered from the sunken *Rebecca*. By midafternoon, everything was in place.

The ex-Navy Seal returned to brief the skipper. "We have the trip wires set to warn us if the enemy gets past the sentries. I stationed our lookouts on the hilltops at two-mile intervals. They'll use signal mirrors to relay positions and movement. Once the Viking chieftains discover the town is empty, they'll come looking for us, and I figure they'll send another search party. We've buried the bodies of the dead deep inside the forest, but you can bet they'll find the trampled ground and signs of conflict. It's just a matter of time before they follow the breadcrumbs to our hideout."

Jim nodded, shuddering to think what might have happened without the warning from Roland, risking everything to sail to Utopia in a boat not much bigger than a sailing dinghy. The skipper thanked John Phillip, then hobbled over to Roland, who was eating bread and drinking from a jug of water.

"So, Roland, how are you feeling after your long ocean passage?"

"I am well, Jim. Fredrick tells me you are a sailor too, so perhaps you are familiar with the mysterious ghost of the sea? I was close to death from fatigue, my mast broken, my strength gone. From nowhere, this sea-spirit appeared, touched my shoulder, promising all would be well. As if by magic, my body surged with renewed energy, my thirst disappeared, and I rowed my boat to the Utopian port where I met Fredrick."

Telling Roland he would return soon, Jim went to find Big Ben, who was helping Tilly change Timo's dressings. Pulling him aside, he said, "Ben, do you still have the picture you taped to the console on the *Rebecca*?"

"Sure, Skipper, that was one of the first things I grabbed when we salvaged gear from your boat."

He pulled the tiny reproduction of the famous Warner Sallman painting from his cargo pants' pocket, now protected in a plastic zip-up bag. Both men walked back to where the young man sat, and Jim introduced Ben to Roland, who handed him the print of the sailor in the stormy sea with The Christ behind him.

Roland gasped with surprise. "Yes, this is the same spirit! Who is this man who saved my life? He disappeared like the mist before I could thank him."

The two rescuers smiled at one another, then Ben sat down and said, "Roland, he's helped me and my wife through some mighty tough times too, when all seemed lost. Let me share a few stories with you."

As they talked, Jim whispered a prayer of gratitude, thanking God for sending this courageous man to warn them. They would need one last miracle to overcome the fury of the Viking raiders who had just landed on the shores of Utopia.

Chapter 60

The lookouts stationed along the tops of the cliffs sighted the two-man scouting party, and flashed their signal mirrors to alert the guards nearest the cave. Jim ordered the resisters to capture both men unharmed so they could learn more about the warriors now occupying the Utopian seaport.

John Phillip and five men waited on each side of the approach path near the base of the falls. As soon as the enemy entered the trap, they pounced, wrestling the invaders to the ground. He was stunned that neither man offered the least resistance as they were blindfolded and marched back to the hideout.

They separated the prisoners from one another, including the warrior survivor from the earlier skirmish, now being controlled by drugs because of his violent nature. Jim wanted to interrogate the men separately to compare answers for lies or inaccuracies. He started with the younger of the two, a stocky, fair-haired warrior named Olaf, who sailed aboard the longship *Red Dragon* with Tillman the Great, ruler of Thormanta.

The prisoner confirmed only three ships landed, each carrying about sixty warriors. They found the seaport abandoned, so Tillman sent the two scouts ahead to locate the others and return with directions to the resister's hideout. When captured, they had just come across the trampled path which led to the waterfall.

"Okay, three of your longships moored here," said Jim. "So, where are the other two ships? We know five of your dragon ships were being prepared for the invasion. Are those vessels scheduled to depart later?"

The captive shook his head and said, "No, we all set sail together. Our vessel was third in line as we entered the Ferdinand Passage. Without warning, the lead ship's mast tumbled over into the sea. She slewed out of control, hitting the coral reefs, and her hull heeled over like an uprooted tree. Men jumped overboard to abandon the wreck."

His voice choked with emotion as he paused before continuing.

"The second vessel had no time to change course. She collided with the first ship, crushing her bow like a rotted timber. Men fell into the water, but the horror was only beginning! Next came the beasts of the deep, the sharks, smelling the blood of the injured and the drowning. The screams of the dying pierced the night like arrows, a sound I will never forget. The three remaining ships changed course to sail back out to sea to avoid colliding with the shipwrecks blocking the channel."

Jim said, "Why would anyone in command abandon his men in this situation? You mean to tell me your leader and the ship's captain did not even attempt to rescue those in the water?"

"Our captain begged Tillman to turn around. We could have lowered sail and used our oars to re-enter the Passage and rescue survivors. The warlord refused to listen. My friends were aboard the second wrecked longship, and yet this madman ignored them and sailed on."

John Phillip glanced over at Jim, shaking his head. "Why should we believe this guy, Skipper? Sounds like a cockamamie story to me. The head honcho of Thormanta leaves two shiploads of warriors to the sharks? I'm not buying it."

The young Thormantan pleaded with both men. "I speak the truth. Ask the other prisoner, and he will confirm what I say."

The resisters escorted the first captive outside, and the other scout named Torvald took the hot seat. He was a bulky, muscular warrior, and his bald dome glistened with sweat. His description matched his partner's almost word for word, and his bitterness toward the leader was apparent as he described the crew's reaction to what they had witnessed.

"Tillman warned us never to speak of how our shipwrecked brethren perished, but to lie and say they fell in battle. If I survive to see Thormanta again, I will tell their wives and children the true tale of how their husbands and fathers died as heroes, and the chieftain left them to be devoured by the great sharks which live in those waters."

Jim motioned John Phillip to step outside. "Sounds like the Viking war machine is running out of steam and morale's taken a tumble. Any ideas, John Phillip?"

"Been thinking, Skipper. Before long, this Tillman character's gonna come looking for his missing scouts. While we have time, I'd like to rig two or three firebombs further away from the falls along the approach route. When we hear those first explosions trigger, we'll know they're close. I'll take off tonight with a few resisters, and we'll be back by sunrise. What do you say?"

Time was getting short, and Jim agreed to the plan. He would stay behind to continue preparations for the defense of the hideout.

An hour after sunset, John Phillip and four resisters departed on the nighttime mission. Thick clouds blotted out the stars, and it was the darkest of nights as they marched, unaware they were walking into a deathtrap.

Chapter 61

Blackness surrounded the band of resisters as they made their way down the steep slope to the base of the waterfall. One of the older men named Lancaster thought he saw tiny flashes, like fireflies, blinking in the distance. Were his eyes playing tricks on him?

As they hiked into the clearing, he sighted the glow again, pointed and whispered with excitement, "John Phillip, what are those flickers of light on the other side of the tree line?" Before the ex-Navy Seal could answer, a high-pitched buzzing noise, like a hoard of angry wasps, came at them from all sides.

Spears sliced through the chests of the two resisters in front, and a third fell with arrows embedded in his throat and heart. John Phillip raised his rifle to fire, but no human target appeared, only more flickering lights. As he turned to scan behind him, an arrow slammed into his hip, a second into his stomach, another grazing his cheek. Crying out in pain, he fell to his knees, then crumpled face first onto the pine needles, gasping for breath as his lifeblood poured onto the cool ground.

Lancaster had taken cover behind a felled tree, but now, in a panic, he ran into the forest. Two arrows pierced his side, knocking him down. He screamed in anguish, and tried to crawl to safety, but rough hands pulled him feet first into the opening. Now, lying on his back, he shook with fear as he stared into the blackened face of a demon with bright green eyes.

Tillman the Younger, son of the warlord chieftain, shouted at the wounded man. "You have one chance to talk, scoundrel. The seaport town of Utopia is empty. What happened to the warriors from the town? Also, where are the other rebels in your group hiding? Tell me the location now and I might let you live!"

The injured man spat into the face of the Viking leader, who pulled out his dagger and pressed the blade next to the resister's throat, drawing blood. "Speak now, or you are a dead man!"

Lancaster said in a hoarse voice, "Do with me as you wish, but I will tell you nothing."

Tillman's son shook with rage as he sliced through the captive's jugular vein, and blood gushed from the gaping wound. The senior warrior shoved the corpse aside, turned to his men and said, "Check the others and find me another survivor to question. I believe we are within a few miles of their hideout."

As they went about their gruesome task, the invader leader picked up the rifle dropped by the dead resister. Where did the Utopians find these odd weapons, he thought, as he sighted down the barrel, noting the weight like that of a wooden staff? When they returned to town, he would present the weapons of the dead resisters to his father as a battle-trophy.

Warriors returned with two backpacks they recovered from the slain resisters. They dumped the contents onto the ground, and the incendiary tubes and fuses spilled out. Squatting, the leader studied the candle-shaped devices. "Gather these items, along with the long-shafted weapons from the other bodies. They might help us learn more about how our enemy intends to fight us. Perhaps my father and his warriors will use them against the rebels when they attack their hideout."

As he stood, his second in command hurried over and said, "We found one barely alive. He bleeds like a wild boar from his injuries, and his breathing is weak, so he will die before the sun rises."

Walking over to John Phillip, Tillman the Younger bent down, studying the dying man. "I wonder if this might be the rebel leader. Dress his wounds to keep him alive until I can interrogate him. Be quick about it. We must find out where the rest of his clan is hiding. My father expects us to return soon with news of their location and strength. I will not fail him!"

The ex-Navy Seal and his group had run into a nighttime scouting party, sent by the senior Tillman when the first two-man team failed to return by sunset. Raised in a hidden compound in central Thormanta, these warriors spent their lives training in advanced fighting and survival tactics.

The firefly-like flashes were the blinking of the warrior's eyes. Thormantan priests created a potion from dried flowers and herbs which were ground into a fine powder, mixed with water, and consumed. A chemical reaction caused the eyes to emit a phosphorescent greenish light, and their night vision rivaled that of any nocturnal creature on earth.

With this ability, these elite warriors could sneak past the lookouts on the cliffs, navigate through the forest on the blackest of nights, and overwhelm John Phillip and his men with lethal results. Now, they were less than two miles from the sleeping resisters, unaware of the shadows of death lurking nearby.

Chapter 62

Green flashing lights surrounded the mountain cave on all sides. Thousands of poison-tipped arrows entered the cavern, destroying everything inside. Screams echoed off the tunnel walls as death rained down upon the sleeping Utopians. Soon, the only sound remaining was the waterfall in the distance, cascading down the face of the cliffs to the valley below . . .

A firm hand shook Jim's shoulder, the voice above whispering, "Jim, wake up. Are you all right?"

Opening his eyes, Roland's face slowly came into focus in the dim light. "What time is it? Has something happened?" Jim swung his legs over the cot, planting his feet on the cold floor.

"I was passing by and heard you talking in your sleep about green, glowing eyes. This same vision appeared in my own dreams tonight, Jim. I believe you and the Utopians are in grave danger."

"What are you talking about, Roland? I had a nightmare, nothing more."

"No, Jim, this is a warning. We need to talk outside where we will not disturb the others. Please, give me a chance to explain this to you."

The two men found a quiet spot near the back entrance to the cave, far enough away so the sentry on duty would not overhear them. A gentle wind blew from the south, carrying the scent of jasmine as Roland told his tale.

"Back in Thormanta, there are rumors of a mountain retreat deep in the interior. The chieftains and those warriors of high rank send their sons to this place where priests train them in black magic. These fighters are said to have glowing green eyes. In my dream, your men walked into a trap, surrounded by black shadows with green flames in place of their eyes. All of them were overcome. Does your God talk to you in your dreams, Jim?"

A strange chill shook the skipper to the core as Roland's words hit home. "There may be something to this, but let's talk with Fredrick and my rescue team before I decide on what to do next."

They returned to the cave and woke up Ben, JT, and Fredrick, and everyone gathered outside. All three men listened as Jim and Roland described the eerie likeness of their dreams.

Fredrick spoke without hesitation. "Yes, I know this story. Long ago, the elders mentioned an elite class of warriors who have invisible bodies. When they attack, you see only green flashes of light. It is said they drink a potion which allows them to see at night with the clarity of the horned owl. They are called *demon warriors*. I always believed this to be a myth of the Norse poets, but perhaps not."

JT said, "Skipper, that story sounds crazy, but I gotta find out if John Phillip is okay."

"Same here, Skip," added Ben. "If they're in trouble, we gotta help them."

Jim didn't want to walk into another trap, if that's what had happened to the ex-Navy Seal and the others. They needed an expert to navigate the perilous paths at night.

He remembered Timo saying the resister Demetrius was an experienced trapper who hunted in this area. He might know an alternate route. The rescuers woke the young Utopian, who joined them outside the cave, and listened as they described what they wanted to do.

"Yes, Jim, I have intimate knowledge of these woods by day or night. A hidden trail lies deep inside the forest, running almost parallel to the normal path. After dark, the stars are blocked by tree branches overhead, so you must use the signs of nature to find your way. I will be glad to guide you."

Jim appointed Ben, Roland, and Fredrick to stay behind and assist the resisters. They woke up the remaining Utopians to prepare for the defense of the stone fortress and its inhabitants. He chose Solomon, with his natural talent as a sniper, to join the search party, and the young resister was eager to take part.

As soon as Tilly learned of the planned rescue mission, she hurried over and pulled the skipper aside. "Jim, you're still healing from your wounds. If those stitches pull out, you could . . ."

Before she finished, he interrupted. "Tilly, you've done an excellent job of patching me up, but I'm going on this one. John Phillip and four other men might be in danger."

She nodded, knowing there was not a lot more she could do. "I will pray for you and your men and for those who may be in danger."

The search party loaded their weapons, strapped on combat knives, and stocked up on ammo. All except the young guide put on night-vision goggles. Demetrius led the way down the path, and halfway to the bottom of the falls, they changed direction, stepping into the dense black forest. The hunt for the five-man team was now underway.

Chapter 63

Thick vegetation slowed the team as they navigated through the forest. Without night-vision goggles and a human guide, progress would have been impossible. Jim glanced at his wristwatch, already three thirty in the morning. The wind whistled through the branches; the scent of earthy loam was everywhere.

Without warning, Demetrius stopped, raised his hand, and motioned for everyone to crouch down. He pointed to the clearing on the other side of the tree line.

Six invaders dressed in black stood near a stout oak tree, almost invisible except for the flashes of green light from their eyes. The tallest warrior bent down and slapped his hand back and forth near the base of the oak. As the man stood and walked away, the rescuers gasped, seeing John Phillip slumped over, his body bound by heavy rope.

Jim whispered to the group, assigning each man to different targets. They took aim, and seconds later, the thunder of gunfire erupted, cutting down the demon warriors one by one.

Solomon took out the leader with two rounds to the head, which exploded in a plume of bone and tissue. The giant Thormantan crashed to the ground like a fallen tree. In two minutes, the assault was over. They crept forward, checking for signs of life, but none of the enemy had survived.

The rescue team removed the line binding John Phillip to the tree and gently laid him on the ground. The invaders had dressed the wounds with moss to stop most of the bleeding, but blood still seeped around the arrows embedded in his stomach and hip.

JT dropped to his knees, shaking as he wept. "John Phillip, it's JT. I'm right here with you, bro. We're gonna get you help, so you hang in there, you hear me? Come on, big brother, don't leave me now."

They needed more men and a stretcher to move him up the steep incline to the refuge. Jim turned to Demetrius. "Run back to the cave and ask Tilly to meet us here with medical supplies and three or four men. Hurry!"

The young Utopian took off at a fast jog, using the shortest route across the clearing to the trail. Jim bent down to check the ex-Navy Seal's pulse. Weak, but steady. Telling the men to stay with the injured rescuer, he grabbed his weapon and searched for other survivors.

Near the edge of the clearing, Jim found the other bodies. Tears flowed down his cheeks, thinking of the wives and children soon to learn of the loss of their loved ones. As predicted in his and Roland's dreams, these men were slaughtered without mercy by demon warriors, invisible in the black of night, except for their green, glowing eyes.

He returned to pass the grim news to Solomon and JT. With a tinge of panic in his voice, JT said, "Skip, what's taking so long for the others to get here? My brother's dying and might not make it. We can save time by carrying him home ourselves."

Jim sat down next to the shaken rescuer. "They'll be here soon, JT. We don't want to move your brother right now. His bleeding is under control and his pulse is stronger than before. Hang in there, guy. Help is on the way."

Thirty minutes later, the evacuation team arrived with backpacks containing surgical and medical supplies. Tilly squatted next to her patient, inspecting the strips of moss covering the wounds and checking his vitals. "The bleeding's almost stopped, but let's apply a few more compression bandages before we transport John Phillip."

Everyone pitched in, then moved him to the litter made from poles and blankets. They carried the gravely wounded man up the trail as Tilly walked alongside, holding an I.V. bottle over the stretcher. Just before sunrise, they entered the cavern, moving the patient into the first-aid center, and Tilly and her surgical team went to work.

News of the tragedy spread like a wind-blown fire. Cries of despair and rage rippled through the cavern as the heartbroken Utopians mourned the loss of husbands, friends and neighbors. The elders reminded the crowd to keep their heads, now that they were within sight of achieving their freedom.

Jim led the resisters in prayer for their fallen friends and JT's brother. When finished he said, "We are angry and sad, but remember, the warrior search party never returned to reveal our location. You have worked hard to prepare to meet the invaders. Each of you carries the most modern weapons in existence. John Phillip trained you how to fight, and you now stand as the sole defenders of your island nation. Expect the enemy to arrive by late tomorrow morning or early afternoon. We make final preparations later today. Take this opportunity to rest."

Weary with fatigue, the skipper collapsed into a corner, closing his eyes, the reality of the situation hitting him hard. Again, the self-doubt and fear that he was not up to the task laid its heavy hand on his shoulder. How could he prevent more Utopian deaths?

"One more miracle, God, please. What else can I do to help these desperate people?" he whispered as he nodded off into a restless slumber.

Chapter 64

Near noontime, Jim and Demetrius hiked along a winding trail and cut through the woods for another mile until they arrived at a narrow opening at the base of a cliff. Earlier, Jim had asked the young trapper if he knew of other hideouts nearby.

"Yes indeed, Jim. When checking my traps overnight, I sometimes use a smaller cave instead of camping out in the open. I showed Timo this shelter, but he said it might be more vulnerable to discovery. A crystal clear stream runs nearby, so there is plenty of fresh water for drinking, cooking or bathing."

With an interior about half the size of the other cavern, the space was perfect to use as a temporary refuge. They returned to tell the Utopians the good news, and by midafternoon, everyone was moved into the new hideout, along with most of the provisions, weapons, and ammo.

Now it was time to put the second part of Jim's plan into play. The rescuers loaded backpacks with clothing and explosive devices and trekked back to the original cave. They stuffed small branches and leaves into shirts and trousers to simulate sleeping resisters.

Next, they scoured the trail, removed all of John Phillip's incendiaries, and installed them at strategic locations throughout the cavern. They would wait until the next morning to rig the monofilament trip wires to the detonators.

Now came the final step of the plan. Returning to the scene of the earlier skirmish, the men set about the grim task of burying the fallen Utopians deep in the forest. They then carried the bodies of the slain demon warriors, placing them along the trail leading to the old hideout. The idea was to create a bread crumb path to lure the enemy into the cave.

Halfway up the incline, they propped the last body against an oak tree, his lifeless eyes staring ahead. Fredrick told Jim earlier he believed this man to be the son of the warlord chieftain. Jim rested the dead warrior's left arm on the ground with one finger pointing toward the cave, as if, in his final breath, the fallen warrior left a sign for others to follow.

If his idea worked, the raiders would take the bait. They would encounter no resistance as they approached, so this would lead them to assume the rebels were still asleep. When they arrived at the cave, they would rush inside with battle axes and swords raised, ready to slaughter anything in their path.

Once inside, the trip wires would ignite the firebombs in rapid sequence, turning the former haven of life into a tomb of death from flying shrapnel and falling rock. Those outside the entrances would also perish from the outward force of the explosion.

By late evening, the stage was set, and the tired rescuers hiked back to the smaller cave. Lookouts stationed on top of the cliffs would maintain a watch throughout the night to warn of threats coming from the south.

Before dawn the next morning, Jim assigned three resisters, along with Ben, Roland, and Fredrick to remain behind and defend those in the new shelter. The rest hurried back to the waterfall, taking positions on each side of the approach trail.

Jim and JT lighted the wall-mounted torches, staggered at intervals to cast shadows on the cave walls, floor, and lifelike dummies. The overall animated effect was even more realistic than expected.

After attaching the trip wires, the team backed out of the cave and joined the other resisters. Jim reminded everyone to hold their fire unless they came under direct attack. The key to the plan was silence and stealth, allowing the enemy to enter the flytrap one step at a time.

Tension built as they crouched behind trees and boulders, each man lost in their thoughts or prayers. The resisters didn't have to wait long. Twenty minutes later, the lookout sighted the Viking army marching at a fast pace, now less than three miles away.

Chapter 65

"Enough rest, Sigmund. I want to find my son before midday. No more idling; get your men on their feet." The chieftain king Tillman had ordered a break for the army of invaders marching from the port of Utopia. The blazing sun, now high in the sky, beat down on the weary men.

His second in command signaled the warriors to prepare to move again. Some men appeared to have lost their thirst for battle after witnessing the wreck of the two longships on the reefs. They grumbled among themselves, always a worrying sign, for soldiers with low morale do not fight as hard. Sigmund wondered if the warlord had gone mad, thinking only of revenge without regard for those loyal to him.

As the invaders approached the base of the giant waterfall, they found three dead demon warriors. Tillman screamed in rage as he knelt to stare into the lifeless eyes of the sons of his fellow chieftains. "They will pay for this, Sigmund! I will impale the bodies of the rebels on stakes, lining the road leading to the harbor with their corpses!"

More dead warriors appeared as they proceeded. Halfway up the steep incline, they came across another, slumped over against the trunk of a tree. The Thormantan leader rushed forward, crying out in anguish as he recognized his only son, Zorn. Dropping to his knees, he pulled the limp body into his arms. "We will destroy those who did this to you, my son. You have my word."

Sigmund tapped his leader on the shoulder, nodding toward the stiffened arm of the young warrior. "Your son points to the top of the falls, chieftain." Both men followed the line of sight, seeing a faint, flickering light through the thick curtain of water.

The enraged invader leader shouted, "Send two men ahead to see if this path leads to their hideout. Do not engage the enemy. Report back to me, so we can plan a surprise attack."

Thirty minutes later, the scouts returned. "The rebels live in a gigantic cave on the other side of the waterfall. We found no guards outside of their hideout. From our vantage point, we could see the flames of torches inside."

Tillman smiled. "So, our enemy believes they are no longer in danger because they massacred our warriors? They slumber in the midday heat." He laughed like a crazed madman. "We have them, Sigmund, just like our forefathers at Santa Maria. We will slay every man, woman, and child. Pass the word to your men. Take no prisoners!"

The chieftain king led the attackers up the hill, swords drawn and battle axes at the ready. They found no sentries nearby. "This will be like slaughtering pigs in a pen," said Sigmund to himself. Like his leader, he too enjoyed inflicting pain and suffering on those who were not of Viking blood.

He followed close behind the warrior king into the cavern. Dancing shadows revealed the still sleeping resisters. The invader army poured inside like a nest of fire ants, stabbing with their swords and chopping with their razor-sharp axes.

In the final seconds of his life, Sigmund realized the rebels had laid a deathtrap, for the bodies were bags filled with leaves and twigs. Moments later, six massive explosions caused the cave walls to collapse onto the warriors trapped inside. Firebombs near the rear ignited, blowing up the back of the tunnel.

Shards of rock spewed outward from the blast, and boulders rained down onto other warriors charging up the incline, crushing them beneath tons of rubble. The waterfall altered direction with the change in landscape, flooding the trail below.

A handful of enemy survivors rushed into the forest, and the resisters surrounded them. The invaders threw their weapons to the ground, fell to their knees, arms raised in surrender, overcome with the horror of what they had witnessed.

One-hundred-sixty-three Thormantans lost their lives in the last battle for the freedom of Utopia. Not a single islander was injured that day, a miracle which would become a tale of legends for generations to come.

Chapter 66

The seventeen surviving warriors were marched into town to the jail cells in the old grain storage building. The resisters learned that these men no longer had the will to fight. They wanted to return to their wives and children and farm their land.

With the help of Timo and the elders, Jim drew up a declaration of peace, and both men held a town meeting to discuss the terms of the surrender. Some worried about a future invasion, but Jim explained the intense fear of the captives when they saw their comrades cut to shreds by the explosions.

He reminded everyone that no longships remained back in Thormanta; all had been destroyed or captured. The treaty stated that future ship construction on the island would be restricted to merchant or transport vessels.

Each Utopian and Thormantan, including the three prisoners captured earlier, signed their name or made their mark on the document, agreeing to live by the peace treaty. All realized it was in the best interest of their families and country to live in harmony.

Fredrick and Roland would sail the *Falcon Crest* back to Thormanta to drop off the captives, then return home. With their extensive knowledge of longships, the two long-time friends would train the Utopians on how to sail, rig, and repair the ships.

The three largest vessels captured from the invasion would be turned into merchant ships, their dragon head carvings at the bow removed, and storage compartments added to carry bulk cargo. They would voyage between the mainland and the two islands, restoring the trade routes shut down twenty years earlier.

Jim would create a coast guard to prevent future threats of invasion. The smaller ships, *Falcon Crest* and *Raven*, along with any merchant ship not engaged in trading, would be used to guard the Utopian coastline and its citizens.

Both island communities agreed to work together to provide food, clothing, shelter, and education for their people. Children would be raised as peaceful, productive citizens of their nations and of the world in which they lived.

Six Months Later . . .

The sun peeked over the mountains, shining through puffy clouds on the crowd gathered in the Valley of Santa Maria. Today was a joyous day, where three couples were to be married, Timo and Patricia, Jim and Alexa, and Fredrick and Catherine.

John Phillip, on crutches, hovered near the back with JT, both brothers too shy to take a spot closer to the front. Next to them stood two women, sisters named Eva and Sarah.

JT's face flushed as Eva chatted with him, touching him on the arm. Her flaming red hair, parted in the middle, fell straight and long down each side of her freckled face, ending near her slender waist.

John Phillip couldn't take his eyes off Sarah as she talked to him, her soft voice like that of a bubbling brook. The older sister's jet-black hair fell in gentle curls down her back, highlighting her face, white as the cumulus clouds overhead.

The crowd erupted in a thunder of applause and cheers as the couples completed their vows. Each new bride turned, tossing her red and yellow bouquet high into the air, and right into the hands of the two sisters. Laughing with delight, they winked at one another, dreaming of two more weddings, soon to take place on this mystical island on the far side of the world.

Made in the USA
Columbia, SC
16 December 2021

51738760R00124